Praise for *What Kingdom*

'Rendered through recursion and fragmentation, the wholeness of *What Kingdom* is revealed like a jigsaw puzzle whose pieces are kept in a shoebox and turns out to have no edges. Somehow both warm and cool, Fine Gråbøl's keenly observant prose suggests the affinities between phantasm, phenomena and what lies between. Bureaucracy and self-inflicted burns – the banal and the brutal – are reported with the same attenuated precision. Only an unreliable narrator could be trusted with this story. This book has gotten inside me, a guide for unexplored rooms and corridors.'

– Anne de Marcken, author of *It Lasts Forever and Then It's Over*

'It has been a privilege to read this extraordinary work. The unnamed narrator's absolute vulnerability is transformed into compelling beauty by the authority and precision of her language. I love the pace of the writing. How, after a passage in which the raw pain and hurt break through into anger, a sentence of clear transcendent poetry can follow. The perfect emotional control is astonishing. It is a very exposing, brave book. It lays open the narrator's frustration at her inability to be heard, to be considered, within the cold strictures of the institution where she passes her days: "the basis of our lives is powerlessness plus capitulation." I was riveted by the attention to detail – it demands our attention, in return; the objective way the

narrator perceives the confined world she lives in, without a trace of self-pity, compels us to know she is speaking the truth. There is an urgent need for the system to be changed, for an individual to be listened to, not just dealt with. This book makes us listen.'
 – Celia Paul, author of *Self-Portrait* and *Letters to Gwen John*

'An incredibly moving and gripping novel... So sure-footed, clear, vibrating, like chiffon or a cigarette.'
 – Olga Ravn, author of *My Work* and *The Employees*

'In this striking début novel, Gråbøl documents daily life in a psychiatric ward for young people in Denmark... Alternately lucid and ecstatic, the novel touches on the welfare system's focus on bottom lines – "benefit rates and supplementary payments, diagnoses and deductibles" – and challenges the perception of mental illness as an invisible affliction... Gråbøl's portrait of the residents' and caretakers' interconnected lives constructs a communal existence out of individual pain.'
 – *The New Yorker*

'Gråbøl's eye is unsparing and convincing, her prose vivid and alive... The narrator doesn't deny that she needs help... But at the same time, she has questions: Why doesn't anyone wonder about the line between trauma and treatment?... about

the relationship between compulsion and compliance?... care and abuse?... between surrender and obliteration?'
– *Kirkus Reviews*

'This debut novel centers around the minute day-to-days of a patient in a mental hospital. Gråbøl, a Danish poet beloved by the likes of Olga Ravn and Celia Paul, weaves an intricate picture of a life lived under rules and restraint by creating a text that is simultaneously demure and porous, with an elliptical structure.'
– Dilara O'Neil, *Vulture*

'Gråbøl offers a searing critique on the way the government treats the mentally ill... Our narrator is preoccupied with the furniture. For her, chairs 'address the night', and this is a vital observation. Our protagonist notices everything. While we never get her name, the reader understands her survival is dependent on discovering herself through these inanimate objects... *What Kingdom* is a wonderful debut... a modern-day classic; one I will return to time and time again.'
– Courtenay Schembri Gray, *The Maple Moon*

'Where less confident authors manipulate moments of rock-bottom misery to wrench the audience's heartstrings, Gråbøl refuses to let ailments define her characters. These setbacks become part of the fabric of the facility, the ebb and flow of each day. Such frankness also fashions a narrator

fully aware of her own tics and shortcomings, who dips into darkness without warning, yet who otherwise observes the world with transparency.'
– Benjamin Woodard, *On the Seawall*

'A striking chronicle of a young woman's treatment for severe depression.'
– *Publishers Weekly*

'A woman in a psychiatric ward dreams of "furniture flickering to life", a "chair that greets you", a "bookshelf that can be thrown on like an apron". This sounds like the moving answer to the otherwise puzzling question, "What if the Kantian concept of *ding an sich* were a novel?"'
– *The Millions*

'Gråbøl eschews the tropes on writing of psychiatric facilities and mental health. Scenes of physical struggle are not melodramatic but rather often distanced in the background, effectively eliminating the voyeuristic gaze... As the narrator casts her eyes on carpets, walls, windows, illuminating an aesthetic intentionality towards space, Gråbøl provides a humanizing view of the facility's cast of residents, and a thoughtful critique of Denmark's state support for those who seek mental health care.'
– *The Brooklyn Rail*

'*What Kingdom* [refuses] to choose a genre, to resemble a novel, a poem, or an essay entirely.

Finely wrought scenes fall into the void, preceding only blank space, or else run into dead ends before undergoing resurrection as essayistic digressions or polemical paragraphs. Individual pages read like prose poems or fragments of songs: rhythmic, opaque, open to interpretation yet startling in their emotional specificity; renditions of illness I hadn't previously heard but immediately recognized, synesthetic, amnesiac experiences of emotion set against time in the thick of the kind of pain people don't respect – or are afraid to hear about out of fear of realizing they scribbled down a similar song once, and hid it away.'
  – *The Los Angeles Review of Books*

'A fragmented series of vignettes, *What Kingdom* is a kaleidoscopic work of fiction. Like a prism, it reflects the bits and pieces [of] intimate life in a psychiatric hospital... Its power comes not from its argumentation, but instead from its testimony.'
  – Gregory Bruno, *Asymptote*

'The novel is neither a "descent into madness" nor the slow path to recovery; it more realistically portrays the narrative-free experience of mental illness... There is a sense of transformation: Marie dyes her hair, Lasse gives himself a buzz cut; the narrator puts on make-up; they begin to leave the institution. This may suggest hope, but such is tension instilled by the narrative voice that the reader will struggle to accept this... Beautifully written (and translated), *What Kingdom* is a novel

that challenges the reader to enter a world that most will not experience, presenting it to us with openness and compassion.'
  – *First Readings*

'Gråbøl, who previously published two collections of poetry, has a lyrical sensibility that shines through *What Kingdom*'s impressionistic vignettes and prose. Nuggets of beauty can be found everywhere... It's the novel's visceral quality that makes it a deeply affecting read.'
  – Lauren Booker, *The Rumpus*

'Gråbøl's narrator cannot escape or resolve her illness, and there is no third-act revelation of buried trauma... Instead, the poet tries to place us *within* her experience, conveying through an accumulation of acute details the alternately mundane and hallucinatory qualities of deep mental illness... By fracturing the narrative, Gråbøl effectively scrambles all sense of progress, highlighting the stop-start, backsliding reality of treatment. Hers is not a novel of overcoming or repudiating. *What Kingdom* is about the living-through and the living-with, about the hard-won routines of survival, and the remarkable persistence of a life from one day to the next.'
  – Robert Rubsam, *The Washington Post*

'The sentences are short, truncated even, sometimes in a poetic way... The brevity is beautiful... [*What Kingdom*] warns of the increasing neoliber-

alization and capitalization of the Danish welfare state and the effects of this on an already strained and shrinking public health care system... *What Kingdom* [has a] thoroughgoing commitment to community and connection.'
– Sherilyn Hellberg, *Words Without Borders*

'A series of short chapters convey the delimited space in which [*What Kingdom*'s narrator] lives as she ascribes human characteristics to the furniture in the room... Episodes of self-harm are disturbing to read but much of the writing is wistfully beautiful and so well translated that many of the short chapters – some just a few words – are worth reading more than once. There is a feeling of authenticity about every word of the novel.'
– Declan O'Driscoll, *The Irish Times*

'Utterly original in its poetical precision. Clinically clear with restrained panic... The at once gracefully poetic and unsentimental tone renders Gråbøl's novel into an experience... of mental illness one could keep quoting from.'
– *Information*

'A poetic and well-composed debut novel that critically takes on the way we view mental illness... There is a lot here to think about and discuss.'
– *Litteratursiden*

'In Fine Gråbøl's vital contemporary novel, the mind is kept just above water... Her portrayal of

this inner tension is incredibly nuanced and highly sensitive... The novel is both poetic and matter of fact. Heartbreaking and critical. Complex, in other words – just as life is.'
– Bogforum Debut Prize Jury, Winner

What Kingdom

Fine Gråbøl

Translated from Danish
by Martin Aitken

Lolli Editions
London

For Viktor

There's a room where the light won't find you
Holding hands while the walls come tumbling down

– 'Everybody Wants to Rule the World', Tears for Fears

§ § §
Sweet Corridor Law

Of all the hours of day and night I like the earliest morning best. That space of time that's neither one nor the other. When 5am comes round I can let my shoulders drop and see the day in front of me. I can arrange my thoughts in rows, and manage them like that. But at night they tumble like gulls around stale bread in a greasy town. I hear their wings flap, but I can't predict their course. Waheed keeps 50 Cent turned up loud in the night. Perhaps that's how he tries to trick his thoughts into changing direction. Often, the thud of the bass makes the floor in my room vibrate. He sleeps all day, wakes up around 10pm, then turns his music on. The walls are so thin you'd think we were sharing the same room or a dormitory. I got myself some earplugs and have complained to the evening shift. If I run into Waheed in the corridor in the daytime, I fume at him. He skips past, gives me an adoring look and says hi. I say hi back, but my eyes are looking right past him at a point somewhere behind his head. I try to walk as linearly as possible. I don't like sideways movements, the same as I don't like sudden emotional leaps, a car driving over a ball in the street. My daily routines are crucial to my survival. Heart in heart, where are we going.

We've been accommodated in this building, high above the ground, in rooms containing many different objects. I can hear what Waheed's doing on the floor below me more than what Sara's doing in the room next door. I never hear Lasse, Hector, or Marie, but their rooms are further down the corridor. We've been assigned accommodation in accordance with §107, a temporary accommodation offer for young adults between the ages of eighteen and thirty. The other floors, from first to fourth, come under §108, permanent accommodation. I have no plants, out of principle I own nothing that might die, which is a challenge, because what lives for ever, I don't know. Sara owns loads of stuff and often needs help from the staff to sort it all out, tidy up, put things in their proper places. Her shoes are lined up in a row by the door; she has a beige bedspread with a pattern on it. I don't know what Waheed's room looks like. I imagine a settee, a thick rug. All I know is he's got a speaker, or more likely two. The floors of the residential facility are much the same: between five and ten accommodation units, an office for the staff, a communal recreation room, a communal kitchen, balconies for the smokers, shiny linoleum flooring. The same number of whiteboards for everyone. The corridor of the young people's section has been nicened up with a *Lord of the Rings* poster, an armchair, and some potted palms. Not much furniture in the recreation room or the kitchen. Furniture can be noisy, so here we make do with less.

And because I never sleep at night and never sleep during the day either, I often look in on the night shift on the ground floor. You can get a cup of tea or smoke a cigarette with other sleepless residents from all floors of the building. Most of those who work the night shift have been given a course in NADA, a type of acupuncture where you get about ten needles stuck in your ears, in the back of your neck, sometimes in your little finger too, as an alternative to benzodiazepines, for example, a depressant. The night shift can unlock the fitness room for you as well, where besides the fitness apparatus there's a massage chair. Hardly anything ever happens at night, not really, most of the residents tend to be asleep and the ones in need of extra support in the form of medication or other physical help have already been worked into the rosters. Often there'll be four members of staff on the night shift, all with alarms in their belts, a different kind of social pedagogue than the ones who work days. They possess a hardness that shouldn't be mistaken for coldness or not caring, it's more an expression of practised care. Although I can go down and visit the night shift on the ground floor, it's not supposed to be a drop-in centre; the night is for sleepers and as far as possible I have to adapt my rhythm to respect that. If we need NADA, all we have to do is phone and they'll come up to your room. I like Mark the best, he's beautiful and strong, with kind blue eyes. Mark used to be a boxer and comes from Kalundborg; he's bald and wears a long beard and the sort of clothes that are meant for the outdoor life. If Mark isn't on shift, I won't have anyone else come up. Occasionally I'll fall asleep with the needles in, but then Mark will return during the night and remove them one by one without waking me up. I might sometimes wake up, but if I do, I never let on and instead savour the quiet way he lifts my head, his careful fingers as they extract the needles, the little dabs with cotton wool behind my ears if I happen to bleed when he takes them out; the meticulousness that can only be shown to someone sleeping, that careful responsibility.

When Mark's on duty we drink café crème from the machine or do boxing in the fitness room. I've got a lot of anger and noise inside my body, it's the reason I don't much care for the recreation room on the ground floor with all its stuff, its plants and games and books. I liked the rooms at the hospital better, there was hardly anything in them, but I didn't like the smell much there, and at the end of the day smell is what settles it; it's not that bad at the residential facility. The recreation room has been done out a bit like a café. The sound of the industrial kitchen's dishwasher is almost constant. The facility, which is to say the permanent living units as well as the temporary ones belonging to the young people's section, is a kind of exploration into having a home. In that sense, the recreation room is like the beginnings of a theatre piece, the outline of a stage design. Mark will open the kitchen for me at night, if I want. I hardly ever do. I keep most of the food I need in my room: bread rolls, red fruit yoghurt, honey. If I do need to use the kitchen, it'll only be to cook a packet of tortellini.

I lie down flat on the floor. Above me the ceiling hangs suspended like a fluid-filled membrane, density pulls me down and I roll over onto my stomach, drag myself across the floor into the bathroom and activate the alarm, I can't remember how to speak, I don't know what you're supposed to do, it's as if my voice has shut down completely, if I even need it; the staff remove my top, it's soaked through with sweat, I'm shaking, a blur when I look at the bathroom ceiling, the ambulance is coming, and they lift up one of my arms, then the other, and note the way my arms no longer belong to the rest of my body, they were never meant to, and drop limply, *come on, move,* someone says, *you know I'm standing here,* and the beam of the little flashlight stabs at my eyes; they bring a stretcher, but it's voluntary, they say, my own free choice. My face's connections with linoleum. Only after they've gone, only after they've all gone am I able to find a little peace in this room I live in.

You maybe don't notice right away that there are five single rooms on the left-hand side when you step out of the lift into the long corridor. A room for each of Lasse, Sara, Hector, Marie, and me. The lino on the floor throws back the harsh strip lighting. You hear no voices, no electric dialogues from any television, no solid footsteps sounding on the floor; no glowing cigarettes on the balcony. I have no secrets and therefore no history. The lights in the corridor are controlled by motion sensors. I can tell by the lights coming on, and by the mechanical hum of the lamps, whenever someone's coming, even before I hear them. My contact person's early today.

Thomas is typing at the oblong keyboard in front of the computer screen in his office. His office is at the top end of the corridor, close to the fire exit, diagonally opposite my room. Through the small window facing the rear yard, I can see someone beating a rug. Purple lilacs blossom nearby. *Everything has to be documented, those are the rules,* he says and throws up his hands, palms turned skywards, shoulders hunched to his ears. *Sorry.* He wipes the beginnings of a runny nose on the back of his hand, types some more, looks up at me, swivels. *We need to draw up your action plan. Write some things down that could make your daily living easier.* Thomas, with his dark blue eyes and black woolly sweater. Thomas, with his strong hands and New Balance running shoes, a wind-up watch around his right wrist on a strap of cocoa-coloured leather, a dark spot below the moist rim of his eye, a tousle of loose brown curls. He's the section leader here on the fifth floor, and my contact person. They were short-staffed when I moved in, so he had to step up. He prefers being on the ground to administrative duties, I heard him say so to Lars one day, I was listening through the office door. You go from hospital to residential facility, from female care workers to male, from nursing to social education; from centralised laundry system and night lights to conflict-ready bodies and communal activities; you adjust. *I want to learn how to sleep*, I say. *Okay,* says Thomas, *I probably won't be able to help you with that, but mention it to Helle when she comes in on Thursday,* and he crosses his left leg over his right, his knee against the armrest of the swivel chair. A poster for Bob Dylan's *Oh Mercy* hangs on the wall above his head. He sips his coffee. *But I can help you find out what to do when you're awake.* He puts the flat of his hand on top of the leather-bound diary as if to consider something, but removes it again. He holds the mug between the fingertips of both hands.

At night, we are a concoction, disparate elements of the house brought together; in the daytime, those of us from the fifth floor are a small, isolated unit. Yesterday afternoon the Strike Boys, a folk duo, performed an intimate gig in the café, only no one had bothered to tell anyone from the young people's section. No doubt they thought it wasn't our scene; no doubt they think that too much consorting with the other floors leads only to debasement, intra-institutional contamination, light-weary scowls. The building we live in was originally a care home for the elderly. In the mid-noughties it was restructured to house and care for people suffering from the most serious psychiatric disorders, people who needed a home, stable accommodation with round-the-clock support. The residents of the former care home were relocated, the communal areas on the ground floor were given a bright lick of paint and various books were sourced and put on some old brown shelves. A visual artist was commissioned to paint colourful abstract motifs on the white walls by the entrance. The ground-floor café was leased to new operators on the promise of them serving good, healthy food on a daily basis. Indeed, everything possible was done to give the building a new lease of life, to usher in around one hundred adult residents belonging to all age groups, with very different, though equally stringent needs. The accommodation units on the first to fourth floors are allocated according to §108 of the Consolidation Act on Social Services: 'The municipal council shall provide accommodation in facilities suitable for long-term accommodation for persons who, due to substantial and permanent impairment of physical or mental function, need extensive assistance for general day-to-day functions or care, attendance or treatment, where such needs cannot be addressed in any other way.' People often suppose an institution's efficiency has to do with its size: the bigger the better. Superhospitals, supermarkets, supercentres. This accommodation facility is no exception. Many §108 residents may find it hard to cope with the social demands of the place; whenever they step out of their rooms, they'll encounter other residents or care workers. On the other hand, isolation can have very serious impacts, and residential centres are built on social foundations. This ambiguity is ever-present, a deep reverberant tone in the daily lives of those who inhabit the first to fourth floors, but isn't nearly as intrusive to us on the fifth, the reason being found in a simple sociopolitical distinction: our accommodation is provided according to §107, which concerns temporary accommodation. We're not meant to be here for ever. We're meant to learn skills to take with us when we leave. You could ask why the young people's section was put in the former care home in the first place and not in a building of its own, separated from §108, if this distinction was so necessary. You could ask why all these sick people had to be put together under the same precarious roof, and you wouldn't be surprised by the answer.

I was planning to crochet a scarf. I found dust-blue yarn and got started. I think it will be three years ago now, I'm not sure. I'm having trouble making it come together, trouble not just letting the string get longer and longer. I call it the string, because it's more like a string than a scarf; it's in a basket in the wardrobe. Of course, it's not finished yet, which is why I enjoy doing it; it's a project that seems endless. The scarf sees me, and waits. I'm not really any good at handicrafts, that's another reason why it's not finished yet. I can't crochet without looking, I can't just let my hands take over, I have to keep reminding myself of what to do. I forget a lot, as if what I remember has to make way for new experiences all the time, as if there isn't room for both old and new. They told me, the staff at the hospital about two years ago, that I should write important things down before I started the electroconvulsive therapy, my credit card PIN, for instance, the code to my phone, the phone numbers of people I love. Although it's a long time ago now, I still get my notebook out every now and then and look at my ranking lists: PIN codes mainly. Figures, phone numbers. People I owed money. The rest had to yield to recovery. And Marie, walking the shiny floors with her arms full of clothes; I see her, and every day I take a new language from her.

Marie's hair is short, it drops to just above her shoulders; her hair is thin and bleached, she straightens it with a straightening iron, her fringe covers her eyebrows. She's thin, but not small, though her stomach is round and distended as with most people on psychiatric medication. She looks straight past us whenever we meet in the corridor. She's hardly ever on the fifth floor even though it's where she lives, but when she is she often sits over by the balcony door in the recreation room where there are two computers. She talks to the pedagogues as if she's been living here for ever. *Lars!* Her voice is narrow and loud, her words lazily pronounced; the way she laughs is aggressive. Like me, she walks as if she doesn't really care anymore that her arms are supposed to be attached to the rest of her body. She opens the fridge in the communal kitchen with her head cocked, her mouth slightly open; she thrusts out a hip, then closes the fridge door again. She gets a packet of crispbread from the drawer, takes a couple of pieces out, turns and strides away. Marie won't hurry for anyone; not everyone owns the future.

I feel far from apathetic. I make myself an instant coffee in the kitchen, over-fill the mug and leave drips all the way along the corridor to the balcony, burning my fingers as I go. I know what's going to happen today; the birds know. I know what's going to happen today; the treetops know, they receive the wind. No disruption in the movements of the leaves. No disruption in my hand's collusion with the mug. No disruption in the relationship of my skin to the surroundings; my nails know, and the clouds. No disruption in my hands' reception of boiling water or the pressure of my arms. To perceive something; to give it a name, to feel it. Not a single cloud in that fucking sky, not a single hair on my arm. We move toward sunny months, the days will be longer than the nights, no change in my face's relationship to blood, no change in the relationship of buildings to people.

Helle the psychiatrist is here every Wednesday and every other Thursday. She takes care of the young people's section and most of the other young people in the building who for whatever reason have been housed here permanently. Their living units each have a small kitchen and two rooms, some even have a balcony, and unlike other social accommodation offers this one is situated in the middle of the city. But young people are advised not to apply for permanent residency here, however appealing it might seem. Many will ask themselves: Why look for anything better than this? And why even try to imagine living on your own, even with support functions once or twice a week, when it brings with it the responsibility of looking after yourself, managing your condition, your treatment? To all intents and purposes, such a life is inconceivable. We're told this: The day will come, and in the meantime we can practise making soup together. We're told: We'll make some soup, we'll do it together, we'll help each other. We're told: Make a habit of praising yourself, encouraging yourself, loving yourself; you peeled carrots today, you can be proud. After seven years we'll be making lentil soup and enjoying it together as distinct, independent individuals.

What will be next.

Someone's given me flowers. A person came with flowers and after cutting a thumb's length off the stalks they put them in a vase filled to the rim with water. I possess no perceptibly living things in this room, certainly not gifts of the kind that are given to the sick: flowers, chocolates, gossip magazines. They should have been made of plastic, they should have been dead. They should have been shiny, hard and almost impossible to break. But they're fragile, and flutter when I open the window; they're slender, and their petals cling helplessly to their heads almost like they're asking to be torn into pieces. In my room: a desk, a chair, an armchair, a bed, a small table next to the bed. A ceiling lamp, a lamp on the desk, another on the bedside table. A glass-fronted cupboard containing a few cups and mugs, glasses, plates, a set of knives, forks, spoons. Also: various items of clothing, some bags and other things stuffed away in the storage space by the door. Approximately ten books, two general-interest magazines. It's deliberate that I don't keep much more than that in my room, but it's not only because furniture's noisy just being there; too many elements with no immediate, concrete function have a tendency to rise up out of their state of thingness and assume personalities I've no idea how to handle and haven't the energy to deal with. That's not the only reason. The things in this room are mine. That wasn't the case at the hospital, not in the adults' section and not in the young people's either. Everything near me got broken and smashed. Glass jars full of porridge oats, the Christmas trees in the corridor, ornamental candlesticks, potted plants, coat hangers, upholstered chairs, non-upholstered chairs, folding chairs, glasses, glass cups with handles, coffee pots, framed posters, unframed posters, whiteboard markers, fruit, Christmas decorations, baby carrots in plastic bags, books, games of chess, trolley tables, a chair designed by Arne Jacobsen. And I couldn't have cared less that they all got broken; that now I'd broken something else, an object that couldn't ever be put back together again. A hospital belongs to no one, hospital furniture stands out so glaringly on its stage, reeks of scenery. But this room? I need to practise assuming these objects belong to no one else but me.

On the whiteboard in the communal kitchen there's a roster detailing the week's meal plan. On Mondays the board is wiped clean and the staff come and knock on your door to hear what you'd like to cook when your meal day comes round. If you can't think of anything, a pedagogue will think of something for you. The weekly schedule contains other important information, birthdays, for example, or if there's a residents' meeting planned. These are usually listed under our names and the meals we're planning on cooking: *Wednesday: Sara. Lasagne + salad. Games night.* The meal day is an exercise in ordinary days, ordinary life. It's also an occasion where the hierarchies of staff and residents aren't as conspicuous as they usually are. The relationship between the looked-after and the lookers-after is momentarily blurred. It's good to do something with your hands. The pedagogues in the young people's section hardly ever want to talk about diagnoses, they'd rather talk about going to gigs or doing parkruns. Transferring from the hospital to the residential facility was radical, as if now I was going to be a person with a bag who'd be able to relate to the days of the week: *Friday at last; I hate Mondays; Sunday and a nice long lie-in*. The clingy feelings of the citizen. Weeks went by before anyone asked me about my past and present diagnoses, it felt almost disconcerting. Nevertheless, it's not like they're interested in a total disintegration of psychiatric power structures; a de-hierarchisation of institutional roles and routines, or a new conversation about the dichotomy between ill and well, it's more that they see part of the distribution of power in terms of a distribution of responsibility. They see the two poles *ill* and *well* as an acknowledgement of the individual's pain. One perfectly ordinary Wednesday, Sara wanted to make rissoles, scalloped potatoes *and* savoury pancakes; she'd thought of it as a gesture, a gift to all of us on the fifth floor, she wanted to spoil us. But as she stood there cooking what was turning out to be an endless pile of pancakes made with durum wheat flour, Nadja took her gently yet firmly by the shoulder and steered her away from the sizzling pans.

Waheed nearly always wants an American Night when it's his meal day. Although he doesn't live on the fifth, he's still part of the meal plan. It's for the social side of it, and because it's good for the young person to keep healthy routines. Once a week, he hands over three hundred kroner in a greasy little envelope the staff lock away in the money box for him. His withdrawal symptoms at the end of the month can bring everything crashing down for him. A couple of years ago the day shift came in one morning to find the money box smashed to pieces. Everyone's meal money was gone apart from Waheed's, his was all still there in his envelope. A slight giveaway. American Night means burgers and curly fries. The pedagogues say that's only allowed on the weekends. How about something else for a change, they say, like ground beef and potatoes? But Waheed will have none of it. He'd rather not make anything at all.

Ten men with all the gear and shields. I see them jump out of the response vehicle at the entrance. Marie's threatened Lars with a butter knife's rounded blade. He was scared and called the police. You've got to act quickly, assaults against staff are on the rise in places like this. They take her to the nearest hospital and put her in the closed psychiatric unit. Marie doesn't go peacefully. She screams and strikes back, like so many times before.

I'm especially absorbed by the chairs; the way they receive me and others in the room, the light on them in the mornings. Who they belonged to before, how they interact with the space; the greetings of the bed, the mirror, the lamps. The way they address the night, the way they address the day, in what sort of garb; thick, light-blue cotton over the back, coarse yellow silk. Their silent presence when I scratch. It's impossible for me to figure out if they're turned towards me or away from me. I open the window, the air's heavy in here; the draught sends patient information leaflets scudding to the floor. I sit down on the edge of the soft chair, its yellow velour faded by the sun. A dream of furniture in motion, at night. I bin things with regularity, it doesn't bother me that I'll regret it later on. I'm not mute, but I leave language to the room around me. The peeling paintwork, the shiny lino, the grammar of the floor. I put the bookshelf on like an apron, click the door shut behind me, and go out into the stretchy corridor.

Every first Monday of the month there's a residents' meeting for everyone on the fifth floor. We gather in the communal kitchen, Lars and Thomas have bought cinnamon swirls and made the coffee. There's a marked difference in height between Lars and Thomas; Lars is very tall and thin with a curved spine and high temples, fair hair, while Thomas is shorter and chunkier. They have in common the way they laugh, never at our expense, but they may have learned to laugh that way on some course or other. Lars and Thomas have worked together for ages, also at residential facilities other than ours, they share the same laddish energy and the same way of comforting that sometimes makes me think of grace. Waheed's at the meeting too, because it's important for the young person to enter into communities with people their own age when they're in need of such comprehensive social-psychiatric support, often you're the only one under fifty in various institutional contexts, which can lead to a feeling of restricted opportunities, a dizzying horizon, resignation. Waheed slaps me on the shoulder when I come in, gives me a nod, *Wassup!* I smile back at him, take two cups and pour coffee in them both, one for me, one for him. Sara's there already, she's been to get the groceries in with Lars. Marie's still in the psychiatric unit. Hector comes and sits down at the end of the table. Lars goes and knocks on Lasse's door, he's not up yet. *I think we should have a karaoke machine,* says Hector. *Okay,* says Thomas, *I'll add it to the agenda.* He clicks his ballpoint and moves it busily across the sheet of paper in front of him. *The meeting's going to take about an hour today, half an hour if we're quick about it,* he says and looks around the table at us. Lasse pulls a chair out and sits down next to Hector. There's a sense of security in knowing the next thirty minutes are going to be spent in this room with these smooth plates, these hard glasses, these formalities, I crave them. I can be the one to write the minutes, I can make more coffee, until I'm released back into my incomplete individuality. I try to limit myself, Thomas knows this, he knows the value of the weekly schedule, the necessity of it. We talk about upcoming activities, Hector's twenty-first, about going to pick up the karaoke machine in the facility's minibus.

I wake up well into the morning with my top clinging to my torso and my neck tensed up. I put my dressing gown on and my head between my knees, wind my hair around my wrist and tie it in a tight yet nervous bun. In the kitchen I run into Thomas; he gets me my blue oblong pill organiser with its seven compartments. I swallow the pills from the third compartment in one go, then gulp down some water. The staff look after my medication, but that doesn't apply to all the residents. Thomas wants to tell me something, but there's no hurry, I can come back when I've had my morning smoke. I'm heavier than I feel, though not smaller. The corridor is an exaggerated scenography; my shoes stick to the floor, which has a sour smell having just been cleaned. Who put the poinsettia on top of the drawers? Who actually waters it and keeps it alive? On the balcony I meet Lasse; he's been up for a while, I can tell, his day hasn't just started. When he looks out over the balcony at the building opposite, or at the movements of the white clouds against a clear blue sky, I see him unhappy and calm. As if it's just a matter of time, and then he can separate himself from them. He gets to his feet almost without a sound, blows out his smoke as if changing his mind about inhaling, and smiles with eyes narrowed. *Do you know when they're going to tell us about the new benefit rules,* he asks, closing his eyes, keeping them closed for a few seconds, then opening them again. *Afraid not,* I reply, *but I think I'm seeing Karen next week, so I'll let you know.* He picks another cigarette from his packet and lights up. *Thanks,* he says, and zones out at the connection of orange to grey in a brittle clash on the rooftops opposite.

Lasse's room is dark, it could hardly be darker, the blinds have been pulled all the way down. His face is illuminated by the bluish tinge of the computer screen, like a moon shining in the middle of the day; a face perhaps unaware of any transition from night. He surrounds himself with the walls as if to be able to keep them; as if there were no ruins. He gets to his feet to reach a book on a shelf. Lasse is thin and delicate, his legs as short as a twelve-year-old's. A bony face, saggy cheeks. Piles of handwritten notes in various places on the floor. He heard them: a choir of bright voices sounding out. The glow of a cigarette is the smallest torch. Sunlight intrudes on momentous thought. Perhaps a decoding of the room's syntax, or perhaps destruction. So sits Lasse; the walls are his quiet audience.

Hector's hair is shiny and black; it glistens. It frames his face proudly, falling to below his ears. A thick neck holds his head above a short upper body; the heart is wasteland, vast. Hector's door is nearly always open, he does what he can to make a person feel welcome. His room contains a narrow bed and a television set. Hector listens to Michael Jackson a lot, to Tears for Fears or Linkin Park; the music touches his nerve channels and he lowers his head. Like Sara he's most comfortable in the communal areas or with the other young people. Hector speaks English and Spanish, he was born in Peru and arrived in Denmark only a couple of years ago. After the pedagogues at Hector's instigation came home with a karaoke machine they'd found through an online classified ad, he's practically been nowhere else but the recreation room where the machine's been set up. His voice is shrill and free. In Peru they treated his psychoses with exorcism. He grips the mic tightly in his hand while his other arm hangs limply at his side. The town gathered together to drive the parasitic spirit from Hector's body; the devil, indwelled in yet another silent male teenager, another exorcism. Hector sways gently back and forth, *Welcome to your liiife, there's no turning baaack,* I hear his deep, discordant tones as I stand in the kitchen. The town, the priest, the family tried doggedly, ruthlessly over several years, to kill the sickness that had invaded Hector and taken up residence inside his mind, until he and his mother moved to Denmark. She married a German, Hector was medicated and given a room in this facility after almost a year in the psychiatric unit at Bispebjerg. *Everybody wants to rule the wooooorld.* He can immerse himself completely in his karaoke; I imagine he can be heard from the street.

I take the lift down to the third floor. The long corridor brings me a promise. The carpet under my slippers, simple resistance. I could go on walking. A light bulb crackles or chatters, illuminating areas of the corridor intermittently. Muffled voices from a television can be heard behind a door, I can hear someone laughing. Most rooms are quiet, fridges hum gently, I remain alive. Outside it's the afternoon, the sun is fatigued. I pull on the handle of the door at the end, on the right, and step out onto the cold floor of the fire exit stairs.

Someone's stolen the flat-screen TV from the third floor. They have an idea who's responsible, even if the three culprits did wear balaclavas; it all got captured by the security cameras. Apparently they can even be seen removing their face coverings as they leave the building, the cameras at the rear having picked them up there. The staff are keeping it quiet as they try to strike a deal. It's important not to downplay the severity of the matter, but it's also important that the young person be met with openness. A hospital order can have serious consequences. If possible, they'd like to keep the young person here.

It's his boots that tend to tell me where Kian is, the sound they make. The heavy thud of the heel's contact with the floor, followed by a lightness in the step's completion; there's a distinct energy in his gait, unlike the more typical dragging of the feet here, that march of the sick. A way of keeping himself going, perhaps, a belief. Kian's lived here longer than any of the other young residents, someone said ten years this October, so we're throwing a party for him. He lives on the third floor in a two-room unit with midnight-blue walls and frayed blackout curtains. Every other day he works at The Repair Space further along the street, a bit of carpentry and some bicycle repair; at night his boots wander.

Sometimes it's better just to get up and walk around a bit instead of lying in bed wide awake. Day three now without sleep; it's getting critical, they might have to put me in the hospital. I get up and put on a pair of dark red leggings, a cotton shirt, and a beige sweater. I take my cigarettes with me, my phone, and put my key card in my pocket. There's a metallic taste in my mouth as I close the door behind me; I know that sleep will come at some point, that's not what I'm worried about, it's more what sort of consequences these new symptoms might have for my treatment. They tell me it's a serious matter to go so long without sleep; four days max, otherwise emergency treatment is required. It's the same with food, I don't know why the limit always has to be four days, perhaps it's like the weather forecast: after that it's less reliable. I'm almost at the lift now, everything's quiet, Waheed hasn't been around today, maybe he went somewhere. Something uncontrollable stirs in me, it rises from my calves, as if I was a bottle and someone poured acid into me, as if I've got chunks of ice instead of bones; the staff can't let me stay here if I don't stick to our agreements. They showed me a lot of trust when they decided not to put me in the hospital after that business with the open window and the police; it was a relief and a burden not to jump, I collapsed in Thomas's arms, and it was a promise; I cried like a dad, swore never to do it again, if only they promised not to put me in the hospital. How quiet the building is; only old Steen sitting on the sofa in the recreation room, and Hanne in her wheelchair alongside him, the same places they always sit. They say nothing but acknowledge me as I go past, Hanne with a nod, Steen looking up from his coffee. I knock on the open door in search of the night shift. Mark swivels round in his chair and smiles, *Hey!* He always seems so glad to see me; I love that, as if we were just friends.

It's the afternoon and Waheed's listening to The Game, so I am too. The window blind sways back and forth, then tries to turn in on itself. I sit up against the wall and feel its contact. I press back, but the wall wants to surround me completely, like I was simply another drawing pin.

We know what sort of diagnosis a person's got even before they've mentioned it: boys are schizotypal, girls are borderline or obsessive-compulsive. Eating disorders are easily spotted. The grammar of the ill is gendered, but also a matter of economics; the curable versus the chronic, benefit rates and supplementary payments, diagnoses and deductibles. Cash assistance subsidies, invalidity pensions, disability supplements. The fatalism of psychiatry. Our tired voices. We make sushi for Hector's birthday party. I slice the cucumber and avocado. Lasse rolls the rice with Hector. We're taking too long, and somehow we know it. We listen to Michael Jackson. The oblong table in the communal kitchen. Splendid hearts, free hands.

The residential facility has a long waiting list, the young people's section in particular, it can take years to be offered a place, which in many cases turns out to be too late. It took just less than a year for me to get in; maybe they let me jump the queue because I wasn't well enough to stay anywhere else but the hospital, or maybe it was because of my age. While I was waiting for a one-room living space, I made myself as comfortable as I could in a room in the adult section, but even in that period they had to send me back to the closed psychiatric unit, and by the time I was allowed to return they'd given my room to someone else. So after ten months in the ward I was starting from scratch. A person shouldn't ever try and make the hospital their home, a hospital isn't geared for it; what they should try and do is make it bearable. I thought of it as a hotel; not because it reminded me of being on holiday, but because a hotel has a certain kind of tranquillity about it that's quite different from being at home. Ultimately, a hotel may cancel out perceptions of time, and the same is true of a hospital. So when I left the closed unit and was given a new room in the open unit (what was to be my last hospital room, though of course I wasn't to know that then), I didn't bother putting any pictures up on the walls. I let the walls bear down on me, blue-white and angry, when I put on my hospital dressing gown. I bought a pair of slippers, and towards the end of my time there I didn't wear proper clothes at all, only hospital-issue scrubs. It was a way of protecting myself, a way of distancing myself from the unit, even if it might have seemed like the opposite. When eventually my accommodation offer came and I started readying myself for the move, I felt scared, scared of the armourless world outside. I've got a good room here, I really think so. But the rooms on the fifth are only temporary, we can't live here for ever, it's four years at most. A practice home, I suppose you could call it.

I sometimes wake up and realise that what's going to happen has no name.

All I want is to sleep dreamlessly, I say to Helle, who nods quietly. Sessions with the psychiatrist are held in Thomas's office; he's not at work today. *Is it because you find it hard to release yourself from your dreams when you wake up?* she asks while polishing a lens of her glasses; the other one looks more in need. *Maybe,* I say. *Or maybe because I can't rest in my dreams, so I'm not able to rest in sleep.* Sunlight pools on the desk; I have pains in my lower back, the same as nearly everyone else here, it's because of the rapid weight gains that are a common side effect of almost all psychiatric medication. *I know we've talked about slowly coming off the Flunipam, but I'm scared I won't be able to handle the consequences at the moment,* is what I tell her. And shouldn't I be able to tell the difference between symptoms and side effects, between the consequences of several years of medication treatment, my body in eternal transformation? But the system knows when it's made a mistake, I'm not sure how I could have thought otherwise. *I don't think there's any other way, I'm afraid. It's doing the opposite now of what it's meant to do. We can't go on increasing your doses. It wouldn't help you in any way,* she says.

The sun shines in the afternoon and the street smells burnt, it's summer. I've gone with variations of white and green on my plate; I'm sitting with my back to the building, next to Thomas. It's the day of the summer party for the whole building; the young people's section has a table on the patio area, we're all there apart from Marie, the kitchen staff have a barbecue going and have made different kinds of salads, a radio plays 100 FM up loud. I don't know where Marie is. We clink our Fanta-filled glasses together. Lasse nods a silent acknowledgment with his glass raised. Maybe she's on the second floor with Kian, she definitely won't have gone out. Marie walks the corridors daily, on all the floors, she has connections throughout the entire place; anyone who wants to drink and party, she's friends with them all, the ones who aren't boring, the ones who get up again when they get knocked down, these are Marie's friends. Perhaps she's with the rest of her crew on the first floor, where her mum lives. I've often imagined Marie and her mum meeting again after something like twelve years of being apart: Marie moves into her first adult residential facility when she's eighteen after having spent much of her teenage years at various residential institutions for socially maladjusted young people and young people with mental health issues. Her foster family felt inadequate and frayed, useless perhaps, and saw no other option than to leave Marie in safer hands, a firmer grip, a softer bosom, that was their hope. And so Marie is given a place in the residential facility here because she wants to live in Copenhagen, she's bored in Ringsted, in Fåreveje, in Slagelse; she's tired of drinking round the back of the petrol station, chilly nights in a field. But why hasn't any social worker, any contact person, any mentor or psychiatrist told Marie that her mother, who Marie hasn't known since she was six years old, is living under the same sheltered though debilitating circumstances of social care and support? Why hasn't anyone told Marie's mother that the daughter she felt compelled to hand over to a system promising more harmonious circumstances in which to grow up, has now been housed four floors above her own permanent accommodation unit? Why doesn't the social worker, the mentor, the contact person or the pedagogue know that they're setting up an encounter that isn't theirs to set up? Why isn't anyone aware that Marie's mum is permanently housed on the first floor? Why doesn't anyone wonder about the line between trauma and treatment? Why doesn't anyone wonder about the relationship between compulsion and compliance? Why doesn't anyone wonder about the relationship between submission and help? Why doesn't anyone wonder about the relationship between care and abuse? Why doesn't anyone wonder about the relationship between surrender and obliteration? I've often imagined the meeting of Marie and her mum, as if it were mine to imagine.

And then comes the rain; applauding, ecstatic. Those seated outside the marquee must pick up their paper plates and duck as they dash for the recreation room. But those like me, sheltered under the soft polyethylene whose outer surface is now lashed by the gusting rain, can stay put. The kitchen staff scurry to save the food from this sudden weather, but a small serving dish of tough, slightly charcoaled sausages gets left behind and soaked. We heave a sigh of relief, those of us at the table of the young people's section, as if all the rituals of the barbecue party have been washed away along with the food, as if there are no more expectations to live up to now. We eat without saying much, Lasse, Sara, Hector, Waheed, and I. The asphalt steams nervously, a release.

I've torn myself open, we try to sweep the bits of me together, but the wind whirls up dust when anyone goes through the doors. I'm still not used to living in a room with a door that can be locked from the inside, but it's good to know the staff have got keys to all the doors. I hear the rattle of Thomas's keys in the corridor outside, his breezy though by no means naïve whistling; I haven't called for him, I think he just wants to look in on me. I'm not in the mood for a chat today, he knocks, but I don't react, I don't want any pretend rescue action here. He goes away again. I've got a few razor blades hidden away in boxes or drawers, I bought them myself; it's hard to take a disposable razor apart, and anyway they're not usually that sharp. I've decided not to speak anymore; what good does it do, a voice, the hard fabric of my cotton top stains red with the thick, lumpy blood that with some delay runs from my arm after my quick, deep incision. I'm still not saying anything when Thomas comes through the door after I've sounded the alarm. He looks at me: disappointed, startled, I know that look, it's the look the doctor at the trauma centre gives me too, another self-harmer stealing time from those who are really injured, those who are really in need, the road accident victims and those with severe burns. *We won't need the hospital,* Thomas says, but I already know, I make sure the cuts are never deep enough to need stitches, I don't want to go back to the hospital. *A Band-Aid will do,* and I almost forget to take in air as well, but then I remember; Thomas's steady breathing, it's mine too.

I find Lasse on the ground-floor patio, we've both got a café crème. *You can't sleep either*, I say. The warmth of the summer night means we're in no hurry to go inside again when our cigarettes have been smoked; the patio leads directly out into the street, we could be the only ones awake around here, there's no one else to be seen. *No,* he says, seated with his back arched and his heels off the ground as if about to make a run for it. We exchange glances and a private little smile when Carsten appears. Carsten from the second floor who has this habit of doing a twirl when he enters a room, often divesting himself of his trousers at the same time, only now he makes do with the twirl. We look at each other as if we're able to separate ourselves from him; sorrow makes us a precarious we, and we each light another cigarette. Carsten goes back inside; one of the care workers on the night shift beeps his key card on the other side of the swing door. *Those spare ribs Hector made today have given me a really bad stomach,* Lasse says, his eyes exploring the masonry, his hand in my hand, I say nothing.

Today Waheed, Thomas, and I are going to Netto to shop for tonight's and tomorrow's dinners. Waheed's coming because the staff are trying to teach him healthier, more sustainable eating habits; he lives on spliffs and instant noodles, an occasional frozen pizza heated up in the oven, but never anything that requires preparation, time, planning, care; by the time Waheed's got himself out of bed, he's got no energy or attention left and needs to be helped. And me? I don't like going out. The last time I was in Netto I found myself five hundred and sixty-eight kroner short when my items had been scanned, I'd bought about a thousand kroner's worth of things, the budget said four hundred max, and with the fifth-floor meal plan stuck in my head like a really annoying pop song, after the impatient looks of the customers behind me in the queue and the pretty young checkout girl's shoulders that dropped back into repose as her finger paused introspectively at the cash register's VOID key, I ended up with a packet of marshmallows and two litres of full-cream milk that, with some bewilderment, and a measure of pride too, I carried in my arms all the way back home to the fifth floor. I slept for hours after that and we agreed, Thomas and I, that it would be more fun, and more beneficial, if we did the shopping together.

Thomas, Waheed, and I take the lift down to the ground floor; Thomas grips the handle of the shopping trolley with his left hand, Waheed's not wearing a jacket. I want to face the world with something other than my face today. I pull up my hood and do up my scarf. The ends hang loose and flappy. Can I face it with my knuckles? The lift door opens. I'm not sure anymore if I can slip out from between my walls, I don't know if it shows. I think about Janet Frame and understand everything: *The grey crater of the long-dead mad lies empty enough to be filled with many truths together.*

Hector's gone down to the Lakes and positioned himself, almost frozen in mid-movement, almost without a sound, endless poses, silent interpretations, weight shifted from one leg to the other, a soft dominance of grit, a displacement of stones, an upward salute in solidarity with the vertical tree. His left palm bids welcome to the sky, yes, he hums faintly, yes, and could stand like that for ever, or so it seems; he returns home to the rest of us and eats his lunch.

At five o'clock I decide it's morning enough for me. I pull the blind up and look out: the weather's tinged with blue. The night shift will soon be going home, the day shift arriving. Thomas and I have an appointment at ten, to strengthen and reactivate my transport skills. It's part of my action plan, but like most men I know who work full-time and are over thirty, Thomas hates going on the bus, they hate the enforced intimacy and the smell of it, so we're cycling instead. I know I shouldn't get attached to anyone whose job it is to care for me, the workers and wage earners who, like me, though in a different way altogether, are vulnerable to cutbacks, restructuring, reforms. I know I shouldn't make myself dependent on relationships that can only work by virtue of my own capacity to intimately share secrets. I know I shouldn't attach myself to people you can never ask about home and family or their new love interest, their kid's birthday, or their swimming every Tuesday, people who've learned how to protect themselves in their interactions with psychiatric patients but who've never taught us the same self-care in our interactions with the health system. I can tell from the faint light through the curtain that today's going to be warm and mild. I can tell from the walls that they're retreating, but they enclose me anyway. When I open the window, a cool night air streams in like an impending revolt. I've got two cups left, the rest I've managed to break; each week, on my own, with both my hands. I switch the kettle on and sprinkle some instant coffee into one cup; into the other I pour red fruit yoghurt. It's not that I'm hungry, it's just that our daily routines are our best illusions of new beginnings, a new cycle. As if I can build on top of this broken world, these interior ruins; as if I had the strength. Cigarette first, and coffee; then the yoghurt. At half past five I turn on the television.

We can't escape the torments, even without a chronic diagnosis. If you've had more than one depression, you're diagnosed as having depressive tendencies, which in principle is a chronic disorder. But for various reasons it still matters what kind of diagnosis you're given during your course of treatment. Certain diagnoses will trigger the top-rate benefit; it's considered that certain mental illnesses are harder to manage than others when it comes to a person's capacity to hold down a job. This is the case with disorders such as schizophrenia or schizotypal personality disorder, borderline personality disorder and bipolar disorder, perhaps others too, I can't remember. But if you've got an eating disorder, you only get the standard benefit. It felt shameful to come home from the supermarket with my groceries, my borderline personality disorder and bipolar diagnosis and my top-rate benefit, and walk past Ellen's teenage room, her wheelchair in the corridor; her life there at that point relied on the lowest energy levels, the smallest movements. She soon moved to another residential facility where they were more focused on eating disorders and eating habits. As if those suffering from eating disorders must always have a unit for themselves, it was the same at the hospital. We could spot them right away; the young people from *le pavillon des enfants fous*. The young people's unit at the hospital ranged over a wider span of diagnoses. It was enough for us just to be young, that was what united us, almost like now. United in our torment, chronic or otherwise.

Sara's eyes are vacant and dull, her hair is long and matted. We're both sitting on the sofa in the communal kitchen; she takes up as little space as she can, but not because I take up too much, I think it's just a habit. She crosses her left leg over her right, slouches, head dropped forward, stomach slack, as if now she's given up. She navigates through the Friday TV guide, restless, indecisive; I stop looking at the TV and look only at Sara's hands, the way they cradle the remote. Her hand, at rest now; her thumb rejoins her fingers. *Have you seen it before?* she asks. *Yes, I've seen Girl, Interrupted before*; the aggressive caring relationship between Angelina Jolie and Winona Ryder, Brittany Murphy's thick hair and perfect skin. *As if any bulimic would have such good teeth*, says Sara. We see Daisy in bed with a whole roasted chicken and a teddy bear stuffed with Valium, her sweater's baby-blue and furry. I get up and pull the curtain across to make the ribbon of sunlight at my side go away. Susanna is the movie's main character, they commit her to the psychiatric ward for being promiscuous and out of control; she gives her body away too easily to a professor in the stuffy old college where she's a student. She swallows a jar of aspirin too, that's what does it. *Psychiatry and economics are different; the length of Susanna's stay isn't fixed,* the psychiatrist tells Susanna's parents; he's calm and composed, in a comfortable suit and tie. Sara grabs a cushion with the tips of her fingers and slings it behind her back, tucks it behind her neck. Susanna is borderline like Sara and me, but *between what and what?* a person might ask, as Susanna does. *It's not uncommon, especially among young women,* the psychiatrist says, informing Susanna's mortified parents of her diagnosis; it's their sentence almost, a punishment. *Girl, Interrupted* was a staple of Friday film nights at the Psychiatric Unit for Children and Young People, the way I remember it we hardly watched anything else. When I look at Susanna in the bath scene, I think about fourteen-year-old Jamie, I think about Martha, who was there long-term; we each became totally absorbed in Susanna, in Lisa, in Daisy, and we had our favourites too; we chain-smoked while keeping ten metres apart, it was in the rules there; when they gave us leave to go out, we went to the shopping centre and stole G-strings from H&M; we rasped our feet with worn-down foot files, and young nurses tucked us in at bedtime under weighted ball blankets in our separate rooms; sometimes we cried ourselves to sleep, sometimes our bandages matched. *What world is this*, the hospital's chief psychiatrist asks in a scene with Susanna, all turquoise tiles. *What kingdom.* Sara draws her left knee up under her chin, her eyebrows meet in the middle, a strand of hair has come undone and curls around her cheek.

My favourite scene is when they abscond from the institution. She bites a flake of skin from her lower lip. *If it was up to me, the film could stop right there.*

◊ ◊ ◊
Containment

Something blue hangs draped over the chair, the light falls on a loose end, the blue reaches out to me, an open halo, a simple embrace. The individual shards of glass on the floor. A moist plastic bag tied with a belt; an attempt to bypass the body's survival reflexes. Not much blood; a small amount of vomit in a floral-patterned bowl. The wall is cool against my back, it's knobbly and hard, the peeling white paint's like an assault. We've been sitting like this for a while, Thomas and I, without speaking. Thomas isn't supposed to be at work today, but he's come in anyway, you could call it a kind of emergency. It's getting harder to recognise myself outside my room. He gets to his feet, abruptly, as if stepping out of his frame in some simpler material form to fetch me that glass of water and then stepping in again, cooler than before. I sip the water and hand him back the glass; he puts it down on the floor beside him. His left nostril squeaks as he inhales; his breathing has settled now, a slow rise and fall of his chest. Thomas's clothes are spattered with white and black paint, and I'm struck by an acute sense of shame; he could have finished painting his living room, it could have been white. He could have been enjoying a day off, only I can't understand how.

It's important the young person is well enough to cope outside the hospital. That doesn't mean they can't be admitted to the psychiatric unit once in a while, in exceptional circumstances and for shorter periods of time, but essentially it's crucial for the young person's treatment here on the fifth floor that they don't spend too much time away from their care workers and the institution's routines. We think about that a lot at the moment now that Lasse's been admitted three times in less than a month; we think about it, all of us, and we know we're thinking the same thing, but we say nothing out loud to each other.

Lasse comes back from doing the shopping with Lars, I see them from my sunny spot where I sit and watch. Lasse came back to the fifth floor today, you can tell by his hands and eyes; vacant, restless, dull. He empties the cart slowly and puts the items for the evening meal on the side, the rest goes into drawers or the fridge; we're having veggie rissoles and couscous, it wasn't Lasse's decision, but I don't think he minds. From my sunny spot I watch as he chops a big onion without peeling it first; it's hard for him to chop the onion as thinly as the recipe says with the skin still on it. Lars sees this, and Lasse must stop and pick out the bits of light brown skin; this too is how time can pass, this too is what inefficiency can look like, this too is how we quietly struggle. As he heats the cooking oil in the pan, I see the way his hands no longer obey their chemistry, nerves run wild, the unmanageable trembling I know so well; it's not easy cooking dinner with hands like that, it's not easy, *the past is nothing more than light,* as the postcard says above Lasse's bed, the only embellishment of his walls, and when the chopped onion hits the pan, the hot oil seethes.

I can't remember the first time I was admitted, but I do remember my first hospital bed in the corridor of the acute psychiatric unit at Bispebjerg. The light by the entrance was severe, sharp, but inside the ward itself the lights were turned off at eleven and the place was surprisingly quiet. A patient was led outside to smoke, it was half past one, something like that. They made up a bed for me and screened it off for privacy. The nurse on the night shift brought me a glass of water, tucked the duvet around my shoulders. Ash-blue fabric, a far from clinical smell. An almost soundless radio somewhere. The continuous observer, stationed at the foot end. I felt secure; I had no power. Someone shouted. If I turned away from the wall I could see out onto the lawn through windows that went from floor to ceiling. A Christmas tree, though it wasn't winter. A punctured football. Yellowed grass, garden chairs in various formations.

Why doesn't a single one of us drink prune juice? It's not like our bowel movements are seamless and easy, quite the opposite, they're as stubborn and defiant as an ugly child. Prune juice was about all there was to drink at the hospital the way I remember it. We'd shuffle about drinking prune juice, then tepid hospital coffee, neither of which did us much good, though no harm either; perhaps they cancelled each other out, the way the hospital routines cancelled out the therapy. Here at the residential facility many of our hospital routines have simply been carried over, many of our evening activities are similar, maybe even the same. Still, I wonder why none of us ever met before when we were there. Where were the others before they got their furniture and beds moved into their rooms here on the fifth and were able to breathe out behind their own closed doors? They weren't in the hospital, not the same one as me at any rate. The people I met in the hospital were like ghosts, in more than one respect: they were ghosts because they kept on returning; no one knew when, only that they would. Besides that, you never met them anywhere outside of hospital. It was as if they only really existed there; outside the wards we were visible only to others. Yet very occasionally I do encounter one of those ghosts, as if suddenly we find ourselves having slipped through a hole into some reality warp. There we are in Netto, each with our shopping basket of shame, trying our best to avoid the other one's notice, but eventually, for the sake of maintaining perceptions of ourselves as socially adequate citizens, we acknowledge each other and say: *It's been ages, how are you getting on?* You're nearly always transparent in that situation, and always surprised, because often you wonder if those hospital years were real, if any of it ever happened or if it was just something you made up. We look at each other then and know that the prospects of an untroubled day are hanging in the balance, we wander off in our separate directions and avoid each other at the checkout, casually, as if we're oblivious to it all. As if doing the shopping on an ordinary day of the week is the most natural thing in the world for us, as if there's no one in the queue who doesn't immediately see two ghosts in all their shimmering transparency, their theatrical representations of a person doing their shopping.

The beautiful thing about Hector's voice is that he directs it out toward a world that also belongs to him. The corridors of the facility reek of cannabis. The line between the individual resident's private space and the facility's say in the use of that space is constantly compromised. The care workers' keys fit all doors. What goes on elsewhere is captured by the security cameras. Marie won't do karaoke but will often stand on the recreation-room balcony and watch Hector. We don't know how the days will shape up until we start them. And then we love like recollection.

I'm constantly reminded of feverish worlds. They come not as an illness inside me, inaccessible to those around me, but an external one; the fever comes from without. And for the time being the second-degree burn on my left arm tells of my uncoupling from the world; it's not the first time I've poured boiling water on myself, but I've sworn it'll be the last. It's a painful, messy affair, and typically lasts several weeks. There's not much you can do once it's done: the first couple of hours it's important to cool the skin, though not in ice water, which can give you freeze burns. A moist towel isn't enough, as I found out a few years earlier when a supply worker in the hospital's open unit, in a combination of desperation and annoyance, wound one such towel around my blistering red skin and then went away again. When the night shift came on that evening, the pain had got worse and I remember the teary alarm in the nurse's eyes when she applied an ointment to the blisters and bandaged me up before administering a high dosage of ibuprofen. No, the best thing to do in a situation like that is to hold the burned area under cool running water, preferably for an hour, twenty minutes at the minimum. Last Sunday was a strange night;

there was a sense of unrest on our floor that didn't come from anyone in particular yet was peculiarly ours. So it wasn't the best moment to give yourself a second-degree burn; I wasn't the only one who needed help, the building quivered with aggression, and it's almost the norm now that there aren't enough staff on the shift. Mark resolutely took the kettle out of my hand and immediately turned the tap on. *You're going to have to stand here for an hour,* he said in a voice that was firm and frightened at the same time. But I couldn't stand up on my own, he had to support me for a whole hour as the water ran and disturbance rippled through the rest of the section. Fortunately, nothing serious occurred that night, maybe they all just turned in on themselves again, dropped to the floor and woke up the next day when more staff were on hand. I fell asleep myself somewhere around three and woke up at nearly midday with a stiff, almost immovable arm. It takes about two weeks for the burn to heal, and the pain goes on. I'm still bandaged; it's only day four.

They call containment of the emotional register treatment.

A special meeting's been convened, it's Thursday, 2pm. Lars and Thomas have been in discussion for some time beforehand, having met with the section's staff group at ten. We're nearly all present: Lasse, Sara, Marie, and Hector. Sara's got the coffee on, so I empty a box of almond cookies into the biggest bowl I can find and put it out on the table. We perhaps haven't grasped the seriousness of the situation. Lars reaches for a cookie and eats it whole.

It was important to us that you were all here, says Thomas and clears his throat with a hand in front of his mouth, the smallest expulsion. *This hasn't been an easy decision for us to make,* he says, leaning forward over the table and looking at each of us in turn; we still have no idea what this is all about. Lasse sits down on the sofa to listen from there instead, there's not much room at the table, but everyone's quiet and attentive. I don't know where Waheed is. There's extra staff in today, but they're in the office. Maybe he's not up yet, or maybe he has an appointment with the social worker. *But as you all know, the executive has been making some administrative decisions of late that we don't believe to be in the best interests of either yourselves or the section as a whole.* Lars nods without speaking and then winks at me abruptly, his mouth curls into a smile and I smile back. But apart from that I try just to look at my nails; I push the cuticles down and pull off some hard bits of skin, and then Waheed comes through the door. *What, not finished yet?* he says. Lars pulls a chair out for him, gives his shoulder a little shake: *Just started, my friend.*

Sara asks if it's okay to go to her room with Nadja, she's anxious about the mood around the table now, we're crowded together with all our different frames of mind, all our different clothes; we don't know how much friction there's going to be between our fibres. *That's absolutely okay, Sara, and now I'll get to the point so we can all stretch our legs*, says Thomas and stretches his own, crosses his left leg over his right, at the same time shoving his chair slightly back from the table. *I want you to know that I've done all I could for this not to happen, but as from the first of August I'll be stepping down as contact person and section leader here.* This is what he says, his eyes glaze over and his voice is stringy and feeble. And I get to my feet; not for fear of being overwhelmed by something outside myself, but because I know the waves, the torment, the namelessness, the patent deceit of the walls. I leave the room, but Thomas comes after me, and from the staff office three pedagogues do likewise. They know before it happens, they anticipate when it's going to start and how they're going to nip it in the bud, it's their job, that anticipation. *We can't leave you on your own now,* they say, and the sun beats down outside. I hardly ever want to be on my own, but I want to be now, I want to be on my own with my grief, so I fling open the door onto the back staircase, but they're still coming after me. I run down to the third floor, out into the corridor there, and still they're coming. I take the big stairs, hurtle down past the first floor, all I want is to get out into the open, into the sun, and as I reach the ground floor Mark appears. He throws his arms around me and I elbow him in the stomach, but he holds me tight and calls for assistance from the device on his belt. More care workers appear, even some I don't know. I manage to headbutt someone, I can't see who, all I can see is a blurring together of the facility's beige and dark red colours; I kick out and knock over a big plant pot with my shin, soil tumbles out over the pedagogues' shoes and ankles; I writhe and squirm, ten arms around me that grip me tight. The ground floor smells of thin gravy and I kick Mark in the side, but he's unflinching, solid as a stone monument, and I'm wrestled to the floor. The ceiling comes brutally into my field of vision. Mark hauls me into the lift.

Mark's sitting in a corner of the room playing Wordfeud. Through the window I see the sky above the roof as a column that's going to suck us up. I eat a plum, the taste is anonymous; I place the stone on the table next to me. Sometimes my shoulders dislocate, as if they want to vacate the space between my neck and back; I throw up in the kitchen's biggest pot. I'm so tired. I light a cigarette and it crackles. It's windy outside in the early evening light, a curtain of grey behind the buildings. I put on a pair of comfy fleece trousers and a pale yellow sweater, as if clothes could alter the evening's circumstances; like make my condition be just a simple case of the flu or maybe a nasty throat infection. Would I ever notice if I came down with those kinds of symptoms. Or would they simply be dismissed as yet another side effect of the medication. *It's good to get some air in*, says Mark. The ash of my cigarette disintegrates into the wind, mingles with the dancing dust, a traveller's gesticulations. I grip the headboard, a pathetic form of stability. As if it was never going to be anything else but summer.

It seems significant, in more ways than one, that the psychiatric care worker's clothes aren't those of the hospital; no white coat, no medication-blue trousers, just a normal outfit, a normal uniform. But still you're never in doubt as to who's the care worker and who's the patient, even if the clothes are no giveaway. Tanja from the unit's open section always wore high heels and if someone sounded the alarm for assistance she'd often be the one who ran fastest, you'd never have thought so, not in those shoes. But it doesn't matter how hard I try, I can never remember exactly what my psychiatrists wore, whether it was the consultant or the psychiatric duty doctor, their clothes are a blur to me. An egg-yolk yellow cotton shirt? A faded sweater? A thin blue V-neck? Dark denim? The softest pullover? Mark's uniform is hoodie and shorts, regardless of the weather. It's amazing how much stuff he can carry around in those pockets. Syringes, keys, pills, alarms. A pack of white Prince 100s. Fisherman's Friends. A shiny metal Zippo lighter. His season ticket for the train. A kid's orange hair tie.

I climb out of the cargo bike, an awkward operation, but I manage. The grass is long and wild and tickles my ankles as I step on the ground. We're taking a break, Thomas and I, between buying storage boxes and lunch. There's a bit of a rotten smell just here, but fresh too, of flowers. We sit down on the bank beside the lake; I dump my bag at the foot of the chestnut tree that's long since lost its blossom. *What do you want, elderberry or blackcurrant,* Thomas asks, and pushes his sunglasses up onto the top of his head; his dark hair falls in waves down the back of his skull. He sits in the long grass, removes the tops from the small glass bottles with a key, sighs audibly, then leans back. On the opposite bank people are jumping in. A girl's head pokes up like a mushroom, she flaps her arms, quick, circular movements. My legs are warm, my black cut-off leggings have ridden up my thighs and I roll them down a bit; I wear them so as to avoid chafing, those red blotchy sores from the constant coming together of skin against skin. My arms are covered with silk; the sun's not good for scars and sores, but they're covered too because there are things I don't want to share with everyone. *I think Kirstine will be a good contact person for you,* says Thomas, watching the mushroom as it swims. *She's very experienced. Knows what she's doing. She was definitely the one who interviewed best, don't you think?* He drains his blackcurrant, tosses the bottle onto the grass behind him. *Would you like her to come over for a coffee next week? Informally, of course.* There are more swimmers now across the lake. *It'll be a nice start for you both before August.* Heads surface and submerge.

Kirstine knocks on the glass door of Thomas's office, it's Monday. I've met her once before, she's got short, messed-up hair and I wonder how she set it before she came out; first she'll have rubbed the wax warm between her palms, then with quick, busy movements she'll have scrunched up the ends, especially at the neck and above her ears, before eventually washing her hands smooth again under the hot tap. Her white T-shirt fits snugly under her short blazer; she drops her keys into the cracked leather bag that hangs from her angular shoulder and with her right hand reaches out for mine and holds it tight, a dry, velvety handshake. *It's good to see you both again,* she says and sits down in the sea-blue upholstered chair with the light wooden back. I get to my feet, something wants out of my chest, my stomach's a warm belt. *Shall we take a short break?* Thomas asks as I open the door into the corridor. Kirstine's eyes dart this way and that, and then, as she smiles at me, she drops her chin towards her chest, meaning her eyes have to look up in order to meet my gaze, a hierarchical choreography, and I own only the illness inside me, the rest is something they take away.

Sometimes it feels like you're waking up from a dream several times during the same day. The taste of carbon stays in the throat even if you've only drunk activated charcoal once to decontaminate the body following an overdose. You shit black afterwards. Thin, oily jets of liquid. Today I'm lucky, the carbon's enough, I won't need to have my stomach pumped. And so I drink it, with pleasure almost.

Other times my stomach had to be emptied before they'd give me charcoal. It wasn't until I saw the ventilator and the small plastic bags that I understood my system was getting oxygen and fluids. And it wasn't until I tried to speak that I understood my vocal cords had been separated by the ventilator tube; my voice was an echo of an organ, it uttered only suggestion. I understood I had to be emptied, I understood that was what the tube was for that went from my throat down through my food pipe and into my stomach: to empty me. I saw the room that surrounded me, the walls and the big windows, the view that told me how high up we were, the pale imprints of the clouds, the apparatus, the industry of the apparatus and the people at work, and I understood that we were no longer in the psychiatric unit, this was intensive care. I had to sleep the days away, that was what I understood. And the next time I woke up I was in a different room with no other sick people, and when I turned my head to look through the window I understood we were even higher up than before and it surprised me that being higher up could even be possible; on the trolley was a jug of squash and a plastic cup, and when I tried to lift myself up on my hands the clip on my forefinger came off, and the clip was attached to a cable that fed into some system or other, and a small person I didn't recognise got up from their chair and quickly, yet with care, put the clip back in place on my forefinger. At the collar of his pale blue smock, next to his medical students' association name tag, were a few spots of something violet that looked like it could have been beetroot juice or a light-bodied, fruit-forward red wine, and underneath the smock he wore a tired-looking white T-shirt. He put the book he was reading down on the chair as he stood up. My nose was connected via a tube to the apparatus next to me and I understood that my body was receiving support in order to keep breathing: that my lungs were too weak. At this point I became aware too of the metal bedpan under my buttocks to collect my black excrement, and the urinary catheter to empty my bladder, and I understood that what was fed into my body was activated charcoal, and I was connected up to all the tubes. The days were as signs drawn by hands in the air; depictions of knots or loops. I couldn't understand my body when I woke up from my induced coma following a serious infection of the left lung due to inhalation of vomit after another failed attempt at taking something that would make me disappear. The ventilator at my side was on wheels, like a piece of luggage. I was weak and as soft as dough, and urine left me without control. But that's a long time ago now.

Night is closing in, and with it the time I care for the least. I have various routines designed to restore healthy sleep. The window is open, the roller blind sways lazily with the breeze; the time is around ten and I hold off taking my sleep-aid tablet until I'm sure I can fall asleep. These two hours or so, roughly from nine to eleven, are preparation for sleep. Kirstine knows some reflexology from a course she attended once and according to her a lot of people who find it hard to sleep benefit greatly from that form of massage with its application of pressure to specific points of the body. I'm not sceptical or mistrustful, not exactly, but then you couldn't call me hopeful either. I've switched off the TV, switched off my laptop, I've brushed my teeth and said to myself three times out loud while looking at myself in the mirror, I'm so tired, and now I'm lying down on my bed, in my comfy clothes, and Kirstine is seated on a chair at the foot end. *Does your mum have as much hard skin under her feet? It looks almost genetic,* she says, pressing here and there with her fingers and thumbs. I get deluded, that's the fact of the matter, deluded every night in my naïve belief that fatigue will overwhelm me and I'll abandon myself to it, content and exhausted, but no. Tonight will be no different, tonight is no exception. I put my arms out to my sides as if to make room for my chest to slip away, to depart into the roller blind's billowing off-white embrace, to give itself up to a dreary dance removed from the rest of the furniture in the room, envious of the chairs and their lack of need for sleep.

It's this harsh sort of knocking, something hard, metallic maybe, I don't know, Lasse says, standing in the smokers' yard with Mark somewhere around midnight. *It comes down through the floors and then I feel it in my back like it's sharp and pointed, and cold as ice.* He indicates where with the knuckle of his forefinger before lighting his cigarette. Like a burglar I follow their conversation from the patio chair underneath the parasol. Mark nods, lights his own long white Prince and sits down on the bench beside him. *Do you think someone's doing it to you on purpose?* he asks, blowing a quick puff of smoke from the corner of his mouth. *Yes, I do,* Lasse replies, his voice old-sounding yet alive, and I'm amazed he even responds. *They want to persecute me, for whatever reason. And they're hurting me too.* He exhales his smoke, while I burn a fingernail in my lighter's feeble flame.

How about a nice little walk tonight? says Lars after knocking on Sara's door then mine, a Wednesday around eight. The evening's bursting, a near-aggressive insistence on light. Sara whoops, I do too and put on a black linen shirt. I step out into the quivering corridor and the room doors open one after another: Hector, Lasse, Sara, Marie. Waheed appears from the back stairs. Sara takes a little bag with her and I ask if she can look after my wallet. *Ice cream, the authority's paying,* says Lars and sends me a wink. I toss my wallet back onto my bed and close the door behind me. Marie wriggles into a pullover hoodie, its hem aligns with the waistband of her mint-green hot pants. *Lars!* she calls out, strides up alongside him and hooks her arm around his.

In the street the air trembles like water in a saucepan just before it comes to a boil. A quivering. It's over twenty degrees, a tropical night, elderflower bushes luminesce like ghosts. The cafés are packed with people all immersed in each other, in the warmth and the wine; they talk loudly, as if to the street. *I think I'll have pistachio,* says Lars, *two scoops.* Marie, queen of lethargy, forever unimpressed, leans her head back as if to drag it along the pavement behind her. The sky is blue in a foreboding kind of way. *Cushy job you've got, Lars, I wouldn't mind it myself,* Marie mutters thinly into the air, *earning all that money talking shit.* Lars laughs and pats her shoulder as if drawing himself up to a height above us without actually wanting to, as if he'd ever been smaller, as if anyone going past on this street could ever have looked at us and thought: an ordinary group of very short people with a very tall man. I have to turn back: the light is shining out of them all.

It's Thomas's last day today, he's invited us round for coffee and cake in his top-floor flat with the sloping walls. The kitchen smells of cinnamon bread, there's a glass bowl full of halved strawberries on the table, an electric mixer whirrs. Not all of us are here. Hector opens a Coke he's brought with him. Lars calls out from the stool he's sitting on: *Give us a shout if you need any help, yeah?* I see their smooth faces in my mind's eye, polished apples. The air gets hotter with every inhalation; outside a pigeon perches on the gutter's edge. A room doesn't stop being a room just because you leave it. A guitar stands upright in a corner. Hector's Coke fizzes, an underlying sibilation. Lars picks up a floppy coffee table book and browses the contents; from its stuffy pages, dust is expelled into the air. We're in the facility wherever we are. Thomas puts a steaming pot of tea down on the table and it smells of mint. Sara and I decided the farewell present from us all on the fifth floor, two tickets for Bob Dylan at the Forum. Lars takes the snazzy gold envelope from his pocket and puts it down beside the book. This mild and arrogant room. It's the last I see of Thomas.

It's not just up to the contact person when a new relationship needs to be established, it's up to the resident too. The difference is that one of them gets acknowledged for the work they put in, the other doesn't. I'm seriously exhausted after a day of activities, togetherness, interaction. I lie down flat on the floor, a clenched bladder of irritation in my stomach, and gaze up at the thin, thin outline of the ceiling lamp. Kirstine knocks on my door and says goodbye. I hope Mark's on duty tonight. Those of us with no place to live and no place to die end up in this trial home, this impermanent halfway house. My face stings when I get up; it's bluish red, like an internal organ.

Every question leads away from me, here at everything's extremity. It's been decided the section will subsidise a taxi for Sara and me to go to our group therapy, only neither of us is capable. *It's important you attend,* they say, and we nod, knowing it to be true. But fatigue has the better of me, my body is as limp as a wet newspaper: a listless leg here, a slack arm there, the lids of my eyes are coffin lids. Sara comes cautiously into the room and sits down by the window. For a moment I feel her looking at me, but I don't look back; she lights a cigarette and opens the window, blows the smoke outside. *I've brought you some coffee,* she says, *it's here on the table.* Her gaze is calm, directed at the glistening rain-soaked branches on the other side of the pane; she props her right elbow on the back of her left hand, that's how she sits, rectangular at the window. *I've got some extra cigs too, if you're short,* she says, a gravelly expulsion, and then: *The coffee's still hot.* I feel the cool air on my head, gaze up at the ceiling and remove my hands from the clammy warmth under the duvet to rest them on top. *You're all right for time, ten minutes or so for coffee and a smoke, fifteen to get dressed and ready, and then if you really want to make an effort you should still have time to brush your teeth.* She flicks her cigarette out the window and doesn't look at me, though she must sense the way I turn and raise my upper body, bear myself on tired, aching joints and pad towards her. I push the window wide open and light a cigarette, reach for the coffee. Then the taxi, therapy; then the vomiting, and days spent in sleep.

There's a knock on the door of my room and like at the hospital I can't stop whoever it is from coming in. It made me feel secure before, now it annoys me, I feel exposed. Empty cigarette packets lie crumpled around the room. The stone of a peach, mugs with dregs of cold black coffee. Not much daylight here, the blinds are drawn. I'm watching *True Blood*, punctuated only by the occasional visit to the loo and at one point a quick excursion to the shop for cigarettes and chocolate. I get stressed if I have to interrupt my viewing. I've hidden the chocolate wrapper from sight, discarded it behind the bed, the contents devoured and thrown up again; the taste of bile remains in my mouth. Another knock now, this time more insistent. *Hey, I know you need time on your own, but I need to see you,* Kirstine says, the gentlest voice she can muster. I'm sitting up now, the duvet covering my lower body as I sweat. *You need to take your medicine too,* she says, and I hear the beep of her key card, stare unnerved at the screen.

It's an invisible rain that can't be heard against the windows; we barely sense it's there. I look closer and discover them, raindrops, the finest drizzle, a slight disturbance in the clearness outside. But this rain is not sufficient for the dry ground. It is cautious and mild. The sky is dark, the trees in the street outside my window are earthy green and exhausted. It's Sara's birthday, and when I enter the kitchen she's picking cake mix from her nails. Hector sits with a glass of juice, his hair sticking out at the side; he's only just got up, he says. If I say something to him, he answers with a delay. Interrupted by something that's neither me nor him. The table's set and decorated with little paper flags, candles, flowers. Small round buns peep from underneath a tea towel. Jam has been put out in little bowls and shudders at the slightest movement. The kitchen smells of cinnamon and burnt sugar; my hands are my own. Nadja brings a small wooden flag and places it in the middle of the table. She goes over to Sara and they talk quietly about something I don't catch. Sara shakes her head, looks down at herself. With her packet of long blue Pall Malls in her hand she drags her feet across the shiny lino to the balcony.

Kirstine comes down the corridor trailing the vacuum cleaner behind her, I can tell it's her by the busy way she walks. The weather is cloudy and damp, the windows steamed up after my long shower. Good morning, she says with a knock on the door. *Are you ready for our big clean?* As with cooking, it's deemed to be good for the young person to engage in practical tasks with staff members, useful everyday jobs such as cleaning their room. Kirstine and I don't get along too well, I've stormed off a few times and shouted at her too; I don't know what it is, but as soon as I see her spiky bleached hair, the way it sticks up all over the place, stiff and vertical, all I want to do is hit her hard in the face. I know it's got nothing to do with her as a person, but I can't control myself, it's an anger that starts in my knees and works its way up, ending in my fingertips, they quiver like stringed instruments. But I'd still say I try my best, because I need her, or need someone, almost anyone would do. Perhaps I might even grow fond of her punctual energy, her insistence on breaking for lunch on the dot. *Of course*, I reply, removing the cigarette from the corner of my mouth and blowing the smoke out of the window, the cigarette poised at my lips as I gesture an acknowledgement with my other hand. *Have you had breakfast? Do you want one of the bread rolls I baked?* She stands halfway inside the room with her head tilted, shoulder against the door frame. *Yes, all right,* I say, and lean back, stub the cigarette and sit for a moment. *Back in a minute then!* I light another so I can wake properly. My room's never that untidy, but it stinks pretty badly. Sickly sweet. I've got evil boxes hidden away in the drawers. Clothes lie in various piles, they don't belong to me but to someone else I may possibly have killed. I can't look at them without wanting to throw up. I can't look at them without going dizzy. Maybe it's to do with the colours, or the patterns; recognition and repulsion. I see flashes of a different life that could have been mine. I see the clothes sit loose and unconcerned over a smooth body, and I feel shame that my bones and organs are stuck with this failure of a person; at this point Kirstine again steps through the door.

Are you sure you don't want to keep any of these clothes? she asks. We're sitting on the bed after sorting through them at last. I survey the piles: a wool sweater and a pair of leggings in a shiny stretch material are all there is in the keep pile. I don't know how to live up to the clothes I wear. They transport me. *Yes, quite sure*, I reply. A strip of sunlight falls on a red velour dress, now helplessly luminous. *There might be something you'll wish you hadn't tossed at some point*, she says and draws her knees up under her chin, moves a spike of hair, *you never know, it might all fit you again then.* Her voice brightens as she speaks, rises an octave, her mouth widening in a smile, lips closed. *It'll never happen*, I tell her. I get down from the bed and fill my arms from the top of a pile, momentarily pausing at the sight of a bashful cotton hat. I carry the clothes over to the window and toss them out item by item, watch them drop and land in the parking spaces below where they lie and speckle the ground like blossoms detached from trees, or clumps of feathers, remains of the bird that is caught by the cat.

I run into Waheed outside the shop. He moves lightly on his feet and keeps his eyes straight ahead, like one of those jellyfish you'd think are simply pushed along by the tides and the waves. It's the first of the month and we've got money. Waheed avoids going hungry by using the meal scheme. He told me once about having himself committed, how it was a way to get a bed and something to eat during the time when he was living on the streets, when there was no room at the shelters. His eyes gleam, creaky hands in pockets; his face lights up when he sees me. *Hey, dinner time for you too? No way I'm eating anything Hector's made,* he says, opening his arms to give me a hug while clutching his bags of sweets, his diet Faxe Kondi, a greasy kebab. *I needed some air,* I tell him, my head resting momentarily on his shoulder before we're interrupted, noisy insects and a speeding moped. *Thought I'd pop in and get a Ritter Sport Yoghurt,* and maybe some other things I haven't decided on yet, I tell myself, a Coke, some cigarettes, a packet of Karen Volf Brownie Bites. *Good idea!* he says, *I'll wait here so we can walk back together.* And so I step inside the shop, into its air-conditioned climate, and for once I know exactly what I want: I want everything, to consume it all, mouthfuls chewn energetically and efficiently; I want to give myself up completely to quantities and consistencies; to impose deliberate physical change on myself. *That'll be one hundred and forty-seven kroner, love,* the shopkeeper says with a smile, and puts my items into a white carrier bag while I pay. *Oh sorry, I forgot cigarettes – two packets of red Pall Mall, please,* and so we repeat our movements, item into bag, debit card into payment terminal. Waheed's still there when I come out. I light a cigarette for him and one for myself. *I only smoke when I'm with you, you know that, don't you?* he says, concentrating on his smoke as if it were medication, keeping it in with his mouth closed, then blowing it out. *Glad I can teach you some healthy habits,* I tell him, and we laugh so much the diners at the pavement café look up and stare. *Seriously, I can't remember the last time I ate a vegetable, 2002 maybe,* and Waheed flicks his cigarette butt into the gutter, pulls open his Faxe Kondi, and guzzles a mouthful. We go through the rear yard to the back door; everything's oddly quiet, the communists' festival all packed up, only a few little kids still running around past their bedtimes. *You have your key?* he asks, but before I can find it one of the §108 pedagogues opens the door for us, a brisk shove. *You two won't be going hungry tonight, I see,* she says, her head tilted slightly. I don't respond; Waheed mutters something or other. We step into the lift, he presses four, I press five, and after that we say nothing more.

They say ECT, electroconvulsive therapy, is an effective and relatively low-risk procedure in the treatment of severe depression and psychotic disorders. It's never put forward as a first-line treatment but as an alternative in cases where medication has little or no effect. A last resort, you could say, although hardly anyone does, dramatic as it sounds. How much ECT a patient is given may vary, just as a course of treatment may involve multiple interventions per week for a couple of months or a single intervention once a month over an extended period. Me? I received around twenty ECT treatments three times a week for several weeks when I was eighteen, I can't remember the exact figure. There are a lot of things I can't remember from that period. But I remember not being allowed to eat or drink before treatments every Monday, Wednesday, and Friday. It was okay to smoke, I think, or else I did anyway. I remember the tall, elderly man I never saw anywhere else on the ward apart from when I went for my ECT, it was as if he only existed in the spaces below ground level, in the long basement corridors. I remember being wheeled by the nurse and the ECT man, being taken down to the floor where the treatments took place. I practise remembering. I remember the ice-cold sensation of anaesthetic in my veins; suddenly being brought down, letting go, drifting away. Wonderful. I remember waking up towards evening with terrific pain in my jaw and head. I remember not being able to remember. I tried to take stock in the weeks that followed, what effects the treatments had on my moods, my body, but I couldn't feel anything, as in nothing, there was only numbness, the pain in my jaw, the erasure, my own blanked-out history. I remember wondering, how am I supposed to feel the difference when I sleep every other day and pore over notebooks and old letters when I'm awake? There was something both disturbing and fantastic about being wiped clean like that, and I carry it in me, I carry it with me. It didn't surprise me in any way that I had difficulty remembering the period in which the treatments took place. Only then a lot of other things I remembered started getting fainter and fainter too, things that went further back than the treatments; the year before I was first admitted, being monitored round the clock the first few days on the ward, being in the closed units, people I knew. I've read through my old records, but it's like reading fiction; I recognise the person, only it's not me. It is not me. The time after the treatments is a blur too. I remember in flashes and must strive to construct logical contexts; not that it's a problem, I can accept a self-narrative with gaps. But I do puzzle over the reason for this memory loss. Was it the ECT? Was it the high doses of benzodiazepines, antipsychotics, antidepressives, sleep-aid tablets?

Was it a trauma experience, and memory loss a way of surviving? Was it the illness itself, with all its neurological and cognitive upheaval? Or maybe it was the sum of all these things, it wouldn't be that strange. I think that's why they say ECT is a relatively low-risk treatment: they don't know what causes the memory loss, or rather it can be caused by all sorts of things when you're suffering from a psychiatric condition. Not everyone is affected by it like that. And what do you weigh the treatment up against? A lifelong use of high doses of psychiatric medication, perhaps an untreated psychosis, sleep loss, constant anxiety, the list is long. In that light there is no happy recovery. Psychiatry exists on the premise of internally directed treatment forms. Could we not imagine treatments that are instead externally directed, involving the outside world gearing itself towards a wider and more comprehensive emotional spectrum? I don't know.

Beads of perspiration form on our noses and remain there like new body parts. Our hair sticks to our brows and drowsiness descends like blankets to swaddle us. It's hard to tell if it's the heat or the pills that make us all so slumberous, the pedagogues aren't nearly as lethargic but flit about like the first wasps. We eat white bread and fruit, the toaster's glowing red element seems never to wane; we eat our toast with butter and honey, or just plain, the way Hector does, perhaps with a sprinkling of salt. Lars suggests we go to the beach, only none of us can be bothered trying to accommodate the institutional requirements sunbathing and swimming impose with regard to clothing, mood, intimacy. We make do instead with our own clammy institution, steaming and perspiring, and by evening the heat is only worsened by our secretions, and we see them too: what once belonged to the body belongs now to the window panes, tiny droplets of moisture all the more obvious as evening becomes night and we close the windows when the sun disappears. And it doesn't matter what we do, or how much time passes, the season is always the same here; summer, the hottest we've had in years.

Perhaps it was our best summer, that summer of containment; perhaps it would turn out to be the best summer of our lives.

I dream of ingesting: various objects, meals, people. I dream of an oesophagus as deep as an arm, a mouth as wide as hips. I dream of soft and round consistencies, in endlessly copious amounts. I dream of ingesting large swathes of the communal areas, the recreation room, the kitchen, the floor. Sections of ceiling, tough chunks of linoleum. I dream of hard, crusty white bread that stabs the palate; of uncooked pasta, raw carrots. Long and beautiful throats. I dream of ingesting the brittle glass of the neon tubes.

I dream of skin as smooth as pasture.

Every exit of the building leads back in; behind every door I open is another staircase or another lino-covered corridor leading to another closed door and another sensor light that comes on when I lift my hand or breathe or step back; and if I do find my way to the lift, it takes me down into the basement where again and again I run into Lasse with the milky white eyes and unravelled hands; and if at last I come to the ground floor and step out onto the damp flagstones of the patio, the brick wall that surrounds the outdoor area is now higher and thicker than before and I must sit down on the bench with Waheed and Kian, gaze up at something that looks like a cosmic storm, light a cigarette for the three of us, and try to blow the smoke only one way: up.

◊ ◊ ◊
Secrets

We go in and out of each other's rooms all the time, open a door and lie down on a sofa bed, watch TV or sit with a jigsaw puzzle; we water the plants and bake bread, lean against the walls as if to make a physical contact apparent; we open a packet of cigarettes with the same restless ease, we look at each other's bloated stomachs and wink secretively. We increase our medications, decrease our medications, discontinue our medications and start all over again; we take Oxapax and laugh at the psychiatrists; we try to die in different ways, while life and the section and the system keep us here; we seldom cry; we drink beer on the patio on Fridays; we hear the favourite music of the infirm old people on the ground floor. We say hello to the cleaning assistant, Ahmed; we try to understand our medication plans; we draw up schedules detailing our entire lives; a meal plan, a week plan, a breakdown of our challenging behaviour; we write things down when we suffer anxiety attacks, what happened before and what happened after; we prepare budgets and tear them up in sheer fright when the job centre phones; we're on the sick and incapacitated; we swap clothes and borrow each other's shoes; we plan our summer holidays in the section's caravan and never see it through; we open the fridge and close it again. We take up boxing and we start a band; we sew a cushion cover and attend a yoga session; we participate in group therapy, in cognitive therapy, in psychotherapy, in dialectic behavioural therapy; we go for a psychoeducation appointment and suffer an anxiety attack on the sidewalk outside; we have no other option but trust; we bury our hands in the soft folds of our face and will never be the same; we eat thin cookies at night in each other's rooms, smoke another cigarette, and our mouths become dry.

We can't be sure this organism will carry on existing. It's hard to keep going without heft. Yesterday a plant caught fire on the balcony, everything's so drained and dry. Kian's footsteps in the corridor. He crouches down to wipe the toe of his boot with his sleeve, diminishing in size, shrinking is what it looks like from here. He gets to his feet like a ball of paper uncrumpling and smooths himself down; our eyes meet and we each lift a hand slowly in a form of acknowledgement. In the corridor we moisten our lips and scrape the grease from our skin; we daub the walls to keep the building in balance.

Sara pours the hair dye into a lavender-coloured mixing bowl and puts on a pair of disposable plastic gloves. Marie wants her hair done red and is sitting at one end of the table in the kitchen; they've been allowed to do it in the communal area. *It's all different lengths,* Sara says, holding up tufts, massaging, rubbing the thin wet ends between her fingertips, parting the hair into sections, exposing Marie's scalp, pink and dry. *I've been a bit restless, if you know what I mean, I've put on twenty kilos in the space of two months, seriously, everyone said Abilify makes you lose weight and look what happens,* Marie says, and closes her eyes as Sara massages her neck. *It doesn't matter what I'm on, it makes me fat, so now I'm dying my hair instead of buying clothes.* Sara nods as she dips her fingers into the red dye and begins to slowly apply the colour, starting with the roots and working her way towards the ends. She tries her best not to dye Marie's ears, but it's hard to avoid the odd spot here and there. After massaging the colour into the porridgy mass of hair, Sara emits a quiet *there*, removes her gloves and drops them into the bin. Now it needs to be left for half an hour. She cuts an eight-litre freezer bag down the middle and covers Marie's red crown with it, a thin elastic band to keep it in place. *Let's go and have a smoke,* she then says, and offers both Marie and me a long blue Pall Mall.

The midges are everywhere, you can't get away from them. We sleep with the windows open, the heat of this late summer's unbearable; but open windows let the midges in, they whirl themselves into thick swarms you can put your arm through. Some think the midges come because we're close to water, others think it's because we're high up. This morning Hector woke with his eye swollen shut, he'd been bitten that much in the night; later Waheed emerged with an ear the size of a fist. We prepare an ointment of eucalyptus and olive oil and make ourselves slippery-smooth when night comes. We hang airy lengths of cheesecloth in front of the windows, tie knots in the ends, lie on our beds and look at them hanging pale in the fading light, watch them swell out and sink back with the breeze. We keep our clothes on, wear gloves and hats, the thinnest we can find, yet none of us escapes, we're all bitten to death. We walk the corridors and claw our skin, construct back scratchers out of bunched-together pencils, sit in a line one behind the other and rasp each other's backs. Our bitten skin bulges like water-filled balloons, we dab the bites with cold mint oil and it soothes for a while. We squeeze lemons and strain out the seeds, pour the juice into bottles, and spray each other; it stings but has some sort of effect. We drink water with cucumber in it and rub our faces gently with the vegetable's sodden pulp. We get used to falling asleep to hands that clap the air and slap the wall, the floor; to a humming noise outside ourselves.

Kian and Waheed arranged this early-night expedition to the sweet shop, they're like two overcooked eggs in the car, reeking of skunk. I'm only along for something to do. Nadja's driving, she loves it when the young people show initiative. *It's the world's best pick and mix, they've got everything,* Waheed says, his tongue lolling in his mouth. His chin and neck look like the same thing from where I'm sat. *The authority's paying,* says Nadja when we open the doors and get out. Kian shuts his door feebly behind him: *Yes, woot woot.* The air is dense, as if someone kept the summer inside too long. We could dream of an all-encompassing time frame; the potential of sharing a polypersonal psychosis. Waheed picks and mixes pastel colours only. I stick to what's transparent.

Lasse's given himself a buzz cut, he still has bits stuck on his ear lobe. *It disturbs my thinking if my hair's too long,* he says. The air's the same indoors and out. He moves his head from side to side as if to make a breeze. We're eating caramels. Lasse shreds the wrappers; they litter the floor and look like mould. He opens the window and wipes the sill with a damp cloth, seamless movements, swift, meticulous. We hold each other by the hand because we're scared; we close our eyes, unspeaking, drift in and out of sleep. We open them again and know what's going to happen. Lasse gets up and opens the door slightly; through the crack we see the light glance violently off the floor. We're in the territory of gulls.

From Marie's room a throbbing bass, her occasional shrill laughter, now and then a cry. A bottle smashes. A murmur of deep voices talking at once. Someone turns the volume up. There's a smell of dahlias in here. I can see them through the window of the recreation room, cut stems in a vase, water filled to the brim. Kian emerges, closes Marie's door carefully behind him; I glimpse men, bottles of soft drinks, vodka, lighters, postcards, some other men. Smacking moths, at least by the sounds of it. Kian nods at me without speaking, a secret sign. I know what the future means; a gate opens, walls become doormats, the waver of a heart.

Kian. His hands clutch at so many things at the same time, and outside the summer will not wane. He falls in love quickly. He leans over the table and we talk quietly and at length about how we've slept, trying to sketch for each other the geography of night, the architecture of torment. Are we alone? Afterwards I go back to my room and put on make-up. I spend a whole hour on it. I'm slow, meticulous, it verges on the unendurable, and yet I want only to keep going, layer upon layer, covering up, smoothing out, highlighting, blending in.

The next time I wear make-up it's not me who applies it but Marie. She's taken cosmetics courses at school and scoffs at people who use only one colour eyeshadow, *amateurs* she calls them. Using what's left of a concealer she tries to cover the gravelike circles under my eyes, her breathing is heavy and unvarying. My skin yields to her touch, submits without complaint. She applies first a discreet dusting of colour to my lids, working upwards to the brow bone, then blows and steps back. A moment's consideration and she wipes the rest of the colour off into the hollow between her thumb and forefinger, then dips the applicator into a dark, shimmery shade of plum. Her hands are greasy and smell of hash. She fades the colour into the tail of each eyebrow. The liquid eyeliner feels dry and cold. She moves on to the cheekbones. *It's hard when you're sweating so much,* she mutters with some annoyance, the stem of the blush brush between her lips.

In the car on our way to the Forensic Psychiatry Unit in Glostrup, Waheed jiggles his knee constantly, he can't stop. Have you been here before either of you? Lars asks as we pull up to a red light at a junction I'm not sure I recognise. Waheed nods. We're going to see Kian in Section 810 where he's awaiting a court decision in a case that's likely to see him handed a hospital order. They transferred him a couple of days ago after he'd been held in custody in Vestre Prison. We assume he was allowed access to his medication in prison, though more than likely he'd have had to do without professional psychiatric contact. He'd threatened a pharmacist, demanding money and pills, and won't be allowed out anytime soon. He certainly won't be coming back to the facility. We get out in the parking lot next to a scattering of low-slung, yellow-brick buildings with a fence around what I suppose to be the recreation yard. I light up a cigarette and Waheed follows suit. We exchange glances, Waheed and I, neither of us says anything, but we shuffle towards each other as if to close ranks, staring at the same point in the gravel; the point where one stone differs from another in colour or size. But when Lars comes over, this sense of collective channelling into the gravel outside Section 810 of the Forensic Psychiatry Unit in Glostrup immediately dissolves. Behind the fence, the yard is carpeted with mottled yellow-green leaves; it looks like a pond full of weeds. *Hey, I almost forgot,* says Lars, and turns back to the car from where a moment later he produces a box of Toffifee and three packets of white Prince. Waheed rubs the back of his neck as I crush my cigarette underfoot.

Section 810 looks much the same as an ordinary closed psychiatric unit, apart from the more comprehensive security that becomes apparent when the staff ask us to leave our phones and bags in the lockers, then sheepishly pat us down, frisking us for any objects that might pose a threat, finding nothing. *You'll have about an hour once I let you through, then I'll knock on the door when your time's up*, we're told, and once we're sent through to the recreation room it's immediately obvious: there's no difference here between treatment, serving time, rehabilitation, only a slow circulation between prison, accommodation, hospital; no hope of improvement here, no difference between punishment and help, but adjustment, compliance, containment, containment, containment. Kian appears behind a half-open door; almost a smile. *We're in here*, he says, and ushers us into a room containing a black leather sofa and a big coffee table with an empty vase on it and a couple of glossy magazines. A staff member provides us with coffee, sour, bitter-tasting. Waheed hovers near the door with his hands in his pockets. *Aren't you going to sit down,* Lars says, putting the box of Toffifee out on the table that separates us. *Why do you think I'm standing over here,*

Waheed replies. We hear voices behind the door, a quiet exchange and then they're gone. We polish off the whole box in less than fifteen minutes. Kian taps a cigarette on the table.

In the recreation room at the end of the corridor Lasse is sitting at the computer scrolling through long blog posts with enlarged thin fonts; about indigo children and astral bodies, the harmful properties of water, meditation exercises, breathing exercises; about being a cork in the sea, about being a clam stuck to the body of someone's wife. Hector sings 'Numb' by Linkin Park, he's mastered it now. The national citizens' portal says that Lasse's login authentication doesn't exist. He stares at the screen in apathy. Then Hector sings 'Man in the Mirror' by Michael Jackson and the clouds zip across the sky when I look up. *As I turn up the collar/ on my favourite winter coat/ this wind is blowing my mind.* Lasse takes his hand off the mouse and swivels round. The sunlight reveals the fingermarks on the computer screen. Almost in unison we get to our feet, Lasse and I, we go over to Hector and join in: *You can't close your/ your/ your/ your mind.* We look at the TV screen, white text on a dark background, the light displays its dust, and we see ourselves reflected, Lasse, Hector and me, we see ourselves standing there, our vertical figures, radiant. *Stand up! Stand up! Stand up and lift yourself/ Now.*

Waheed's back after a brief spell in hospital, his anger bristles on his skin. He comes toward me in the corridor. I see his bare arms, soft flesh spiked with thin dark hairs, his hands hidden in his pockets. His face is turned inwards, its lines severe, until his eyes latch onto mine and it folds out, loosens laboriously in a series of movements. We bear our weapons tensely.

We hardly have time to get used to their expressions before the faces assume new forms. Nor do we have our hands in common, mine are angular, fingers the same width on either side of the joints, whereas Waheed's are supple, slender and thinner where the nail begins; they rest on the table like fresh pasta laid out to dry. This is the way our hands look, as if they're waiting for something. Just as we can distinguish faces, we can distinguish those of us who were ill before the new social reforms from those who weren't until after. It wasn't just fortunate, but in every respect vital that Waheed was awarded his pension, that someone noticed him and officially deemed him to be incapacitated and unfit for work. There wouldn't have been much chance today. His soft trousers crackle with electricity, as if they're about to burst into flames. I prefer to wear fabrics that don't generate static, it's a sort of principle of mine, one of many. What's a disability pension anyway, other than the promise of a minimum of stability, a narrow rug, the possibility of grass in a crumbling monument.

I see Lasse come out of his room. I'm playing solitaire at the table in the kitchen. He comes in and his arms are as long as nerves. I watch him take a glass from the cupboard and fill some squash in it, topping up with water from the tap. I stretch my mouth into a smile. He drinks half the glass while standing at the sink, then comes over to the table and sits down with his legs apart. His shoulders are hunched, but his neck is extended; he looks at me with his eyebrows aloft, mouth open, eyes barely blinking, red eyes, sparse, mangy beard; he smells of something like an old tobacco pipe and stomach acid, boiled meat. He leans across, his chest touching the table, and says: *I've set myself free, I've detached myself from everything that's me.* His drink moistens his cracked lips; I forget it's blood that gives them their colour, that blood is what makes them stand out from the rest of the face. I *don't need to worry any more about illnesses or nails getting broken,* he says from somewhere, *because it's not me.* And then he drains his glass.

Someone's calling for us, says Marie and runs her rough fingers through her dry, stiff hair. Hector has borrowed a Michael Jackson songbook from the library and plays the songs with patience on the piano in the recreation room. Marie rolls the corner of a piece of paper between her fingers, softening its sharp edges, tiring it out, putting it down on the table again. *Why isn't Helle here yet?* she says. We don't know where the staff are, are we on our own? Someone calls for us and Hector turns round. *Maybe she's never coming back*, he says. Marie's hands tremble, the rings under her eyes are heavy and dark, like ancient moats. I get to my feet, fill the kettle and put three mugs out. In one I put two heaped teaspoons of instant coffee, in another only one, along with a spoonful of sugar, in the third a Forest Fruit tea bag I discover at the back of the cupboard. An aroma of sweet red berries steams into the air when I pour the boiling water over the tea. *Are we going for a smoke?* I ask, and we take our mugs and go out onto the balcony. Marie's face is pale, Hector's feet barely leave the floor when he walks. Every day we go past the *Lord of the Rings* poster and every day we sense its silent appraisals. It watches us, as the glaring ceiling panels and the harsh reflections that glance off the floor watch us too, as if illness were passed on not only through the blood but also by our footsteps, by hanging around and shuffling along corridors.

Hector's not exactly a good percussionist, he's not even very musical, but as with the rest of us the reason he's in the band at all is to establish a shared connection with a shared world. Lasse plays the drums, Lars plays guitar, the intern plays the bass and I play keyboards and sing. The music room is in the basement, we play every Thursday, and today we're rehearsing for a fun run for psychiatric patients, families, and staff at the Sankt Hans psychiatric hospital in Roskilde. There are three different routes of two, five and ten kilometres in beautiful surroundings along the fjord and through the woods. As they cross the finishing line, participants will receive a finisher's medal and can then help themselves to fruit and sandwiches, while we, Wild & Gentle, perform a range of familiar rock and pop songs. The dark curtains at the far end of the room keep moving all the time. *I'm pulling you close/ You just say no.* Hector's off the beat. *You don't say you don't like it.* But then again we're not dependent on him getting it right. *But girl, I know you're a liar.* The basement is bigger than you'd expect, it stretches and expands with each new room you enter. Builders and their building materials. I sometimes press the wrong button in the lift and find myself in the basement; it doesn't take much for me to panic then. I met Lasse one night when I did that, he was standing in a weird corner. I assumed he'd just got lost like me. The difficult part is definitely the ending. *Fire.* We have to look at each other, maintain eye contact and keep our focus, then make our hands do what we ask them to: three quick beats in succession. *Fire.*

There's a freshness in the air today, we feel it as we stand on the balcony, a hint of autumn. *What a relief,* says Sara, the sleeves of her top pulled well down to conceal her pink scars, scarlet wounds. The clouds attest to the changing season, I can see it the way they glower white against the sky's near-unnatural blue. The waning summer injects new life into the §108 residents. They're boisterous now when they congregate on their balconies, they beam at lunchtimes, shove each other playfully, as if the impossible expectations of summer finally dissolved along with its oppressive nights. One of them even came up yesterday and asked if there'd be anyone from the young people's section who might want to do yoga on Wednesdays if she started a class. Several of us nodded, partly out of politeness I suppose, but genuinely too, though we know we seldom can commit fully to an activity even if we want to. Today, those of us going to Sankt Hans are meeting up at the entrance to be driven in the section's minibus. Sara's not in the band, but she's been training for the fun run with Nadja and is set on completing the full 10k. *Are you nervous?* she asks, looking at no one in particular. *A bit maybe,* I reply, but it's not actually true, I love performing whatever the stage, I love singing so close to the mic that my spit makes it wet, so close you can hear my breathing, deep and sincere, and I love the gaze of the audience watching my face contort with feeling as I immerse myself in the show. *I'm sure you're going to be really good,* she says, and flicks her cigarette over the railing of the balcony, lifts her coffee mug slackly on a forefinger, and goes back in.

Lars turns the radio on as soon as he's started the engine. I've hardly slept, but thankfully I'm not the only one. *Anyone for a liquorice?* he asks without taking his eye off the road, passing the bag to the first outstretched hand, then tapping his thigh gently to the rhythm of the music that streams from the speakers. Lasse dips in and takes two. Hector sits at the back with his eyes closed, his head resting against the window. We arrive at Sankt Hans with plenty of time to get set up, run through a sound check, and then sit in the minibus with coffee and cigarettes. *Are you all keyed up?* Lars asks. The intern throws a smile in the rear-view mirror. *Very,* Hector says, half asleep though chewing a liquorice. I've never been to Sankt Hans before, but there's always been something about the isolation that's appealed to me; endless green fields and no intrusions, cooling lakes to splash in, desperately beautiful runs by the fjord, a slow-paced convalescence, restful gardens. Not like in the city, those sapping, quick-fire spells in the hospital with no hope of any retreat from society, surrounded by the whole world, people tearing along the bike lanes on their way to work, immediately looking the other way if they happen to set eyes on you, the sad life you've obviously got. I've always imagined life at Sankt Hans to be like hospital life in films; the prospect of lifelong friendships with caregivers and fellow patients, brutal systems softened by people who want to do good for others. As if systems weren't contrived by people, as if my own romantic idea of psychiatric treatment in the countryside wasn't part and parcel of the system; that all the patient needs is bags of fresh air and a time spent away from the rigors of the outside world. *It's always such a good event,* says Lars, and Lasse smiles and nods, flexing his fingers restlessly. I open the window slightly and air wisps into the minibus, the sound of the wind takes attention from nearly everything else.

I close my eyes and find myself as if behind my own neck. *Mama, take this badge off of me.* Lars sings the harmony, a sweet pillow placed over my air passages. When I open my eyes again I see people dancing on the lawns; a bunch of baggy-sleeved sweaters tossed on the wind. One person is wearing a pink hat, another has bouncing, shoulder-length curls. The grass underneath their feet is yellow; here and there cigarette smoke curls from their midst, coordinates pointing to some other place. We're near the end of our set, 'Knockin' on Heaven's Door,' the dancing loose-limbed and joyful; a patient twirls a caregiver through the whole second verse. Someone else pauses to gulp some water from a bottle; the sun is at its highest. Under a tree, a small group wearing identical white Sankt Hans Run T-shirts have gathered to unwrap their sandwiches. It's a lovely day to have leave. We leave the audience in raptures. The backs of their hands turned away from us, knuckles to the sky.

When we get home to the fifth floor the others have ordered pizza. They've set the table in the kitchen and switched the TV on. Kirstine twists the lid off a big bottle of Coke and pours me a glass. Lars grabs a pizza slice, *See you, then, and thanks for a brilliant gig!* He gives my shoulder a squeeze on his way out and says, *well fought*, releases. I don't know what to do with myself. We watch the first rounds of X Factor auditions; Waheed turns the volume up. Kirstine sits in the chair next to us with her plate on her lap and covers her mouth with her hand every time she laughs. Marie hurries past in the corridor, a fleeting nod.

Most of Sara's furniture stands piled together in the corridor. She's not moving out, she's having new ash-wood flooring put in. I have to squeeze past her neatly-made bed with its beige throw. The new floor catches my eye through the crack of the door, conspicuous, but already familiar. *It's the lino that ruins my sleep*, Sara says, *it's the lino that's stopping me from getting better.* But now the door won't close because the wood has expanded in the night, it's lifted to above the sill. *Maybe we can lift the door a bit instead?* Lars suggests. He grips the side with both hands and his eyebrows ascend towards his hairline. Sara sits apathetically on a bean bag. *I'm going for a smoke,* she says. Her dismantled room in the corridor; an armchair, a chest of drawers, the harsh light, the shiny floor, the way it adapts itself to whatever; a jewellery stand, her bedside table, a decorated lamp. The door of the room is solid, it'll be a job to even saw the bottom off it. *I'll call down to the basement,* says Lars, stepping back, returning a hand now to his pocket. *We need someone who knows what they're doing.*

I decide to go out into the street, into the misty night, after the guy who fills in on the night shift tells me Mark's off sick. The air is sharp and prickly. I cross the road, stand and look at the building we live in. What does it look like, this tottering house? A pocket hard with secrets? Our sleep holds the rubble together. The window of my room is half open, I can see it from where I stand. Suddenly, it doesn't look like mine.

We warn no one.

We're all on the balcony together, the sun glancing off our foreheads, each shinier than the other. We live on average fifteen to twenty years less than healthy people, those without a mental disorder. It's not just a matter of suicide rates but of the side effects of medication too, as well as high instances of other issues, somatic illness, infectious diseases. The sick get sicker, and no one notices in time. Most mental illnesses are *invisible illnesses*, they say. It's how we hear others refer to our psychiatric diagnoses, illnesses no one can see, but we see them just fine, they're as plain as can be, articulated in our bodies, in our mortality rates, and we're tempted to ask, *What makes you perceive mental illness as something invisible?* Its peripheral whereabouts? The way it's thought of as something impenetrable, pertaining to the individual, inaccessible to any other? Is the effect of depression on our bones and joints invisible? Is persistent physical exhaustion invisible? Is psychomotor tempo invisible? Is the resignation of our metabolism invisible? Our wounds and scars, pink, purple, blue, crimson, are they invisible? Are our trembling hands, our trembling legs, our psychotic cramps, invisible? Is psychomotor agitation invisible? Are our bloated stomachs invisible? Are our bewildered, ashen faces invisible? We extend our tongues to the dust of the roof tiles. Twenty years. They aren't long enough, our tongues. Sweeping measures across the healthcare system are what's needed. Dismantling would be a start. We ourselves do not differentiate between our brains and lungs, they are possible expansions in our encounters with people and places, potentially they are kisses of death, this much we know. The basis of our lives is powerlessness plus capitulation, and we ought not to trust in our organs the way they are regarded by the systems. It disappears quickly in the mouth, roof-tile dust, and behind us the wall radiates light.

So this is where we stand, at the end of the corridor, considering things, Lasse, Waheed, Hector, Marie, Sara, and me, with a mixture of curiosity and loathing. The curve of the armchair, its shimmering greens like those of a wine bottle illuminated from below. We don't have many plants, but the ones we have we take away, removing them from their intimate constellations with the sun, removing them from the residential facility's smooth white interior spaces, avoiding scheming and plotting by placing them out of sight in the lift. We throw them out, the poinsettias and potted palms; we shove the armchair the same way, we demount the whiteboard from the wall and it'll only just go in when we stand it diagonally on end. We take down both strings of fairy lights, the tangled purple one with the thin cylinders that look like penne pasta, and the other one, whose bulbs are as red as hearts; we wind them together into a big ball. We help each other detach the long fluorescent strip lights, we stand on chairs, receive the ceiling panels with glee, the lamps themselves; we lean the panels against the wall and leave them there after we've finished. Another load in the lift, those tubes are going out. And we never see them again.

Behind the framed posters the paint is a fuller shade than the rest of the wall, making visible a form of temporality or oblivion. We pry open the frame, the glass flat against the floor, and pull from it the now fragile *Lord of the Rings* poster, rolling it up as it comes. We keep the frames that are still intact, toss the ones whose glass is scratched or cracked. The rolled-up posters slacken, we roll them tight again and put elastic bands around them. We dump the empty frames by the door of the office, continuing along the walls, leaving them marked with deviations.

We empty the kitchen cupboards and drawers, remove the plates and dishes, glasses, cutlery. We've packed the dry foods away in a box and placed it by the door. The fridges gape, containing now but smears of margarine, a papery onion skin, a hardened blob of Thousand Island, feeble testimonies of our presence here. Are Hector and Lasse really holding flowers? Roses filched from the front gardens of stucco-ceilinged tenements? We spread them out on the silvery gleam of the counter, put on gloves to pinch the green leaves meticulously from the stems. We arrange the flowers in pairs in the three tall coffee mugs we've saved until last, another pair in a narrow asparagus jar Hector discovers in a drawer we thought we'd emptied. One after another we carry our makeshift vases out into the long corridor; the space we frequent the most, but use least.

We open the windows for someone or something.

The sound of the sliding door opening is discreet, yet also disquieting. I've sat down in an armchair on the ground floor so I can be surrounded by something other than myself. The permanent night shift is understaffed, we can tell by the busy footsteps and multiple unfamiliar faces. Mark's still off sick, here I'm surrounded by blankets. Sara comes and sits beside me; her hair glistens with grease and sleep. The door slides open and in come Lasse and Hector, all their mild eyes, narrow faces. Sara massages a pressure point between my thumb and forefinger. Lasse coughs. The heavy footfall of one of the staff somewhere in the background. Hector closes his eyes a moment and I watch the rapid movements behind his eyelids. Sleep is something that rises up in him. The sound of the sliding door again; Marie's eyes look nowhere but straight ahead, her lips are tight with anger, she sits down next to Lasse, spreads her legs, they're long and white with occasional bruises, scars, traces of skin once stretched. *I'll get us all some hot chocolate,* Hector says and gets to his feet. Is that Waheed's fist I hear punch the wall of the office? He emerges suddenly, two concerned staff members in his wake; for a moment they watch him stride away before they turn and go back in. He comes over and drops down heavily into a chair, sits awkwardly because of a blanket bunched up behind his back, though he doesn't appear to notice.

Hector has to make several trips, putting down two steaming hot cups in front of us, going back for two more, returning, going back, returning. We burn our tongues. An alarm goes off, lights flash on the belts of the staff as they dash past. The ceiling panels are discoloured, a sorry canvas. Hot drinks from machines remind me of train stations, waiting rooms; we slurp our cocoa and it leaves a ring around Marie's mouth. *We're getting there*, says Lasse. Hector hums quietly, *All for freedom and for pleasure.* The last mouthful's mostly powder. Waheed's cup chinks against the others as he puts it down and says, *I think we should go now.* He rises and picks up his chair, the blanket with it. We nod. We're taking the furniture with us; everything we can carry is going with us.

Lasse follows on behind Hector, cups clattering. Marie puts a hand on Waheed's shoulder, snatches up a dark red blanket as she goes; it matches her now fading hair. Sara and I each lug a chair under one arm and hold each other's greasy hand. We speak no more, hum no more, there's only the thud now of the feet that carry us. Behind us the door slides shut as discreetly as it opens, almost without a sound. A few birds chirp; the night is letting go, a cautious transition into morning. Marie slings the blanket around her shoulders. Dark red wind. Above us is only the dawn.

FINE GRÅBØL (b. 1992) made her debut in 2021 with *What Kingdom*, a novel which earned her the Bogforum Debut Prize. Prior to this, she published a collection of poetry, *Bone-marrow Lavender* (2018), together with the writing collective BMS. *What Kingdom* has been translated into seven languages and her second novel, *Arise*, was recently published in Denmark.

MARTIN AITKEN has translated numerous novels from Danish and Norwegian, including works by Karl Ove Knausgaard. For *The Employees* by Olga Ravn, he was shortlisted for the Internation-al Booker Prize 2021 and the Ursula K. Le Guin Prize for Fiction 2022, among other prizes. He was a finalist at the U.S. National Book Awards 2018 and received the PEN America Translation Prize 2019 for his translation of Hanne Ørstavik's *Love*.

What Kingdom
Copyright © Fine Gråbøl, 2021
Translation copyright © Martin Aitken, 2024
Published by agreement with Copenhagen
Literary Agency ApS, Copenhagen

This English-language edition first published in
the United Kingdom by Lolli Editions in 2024,
and by Archipelago Books in the USA

The right of Fine Gråbøl to be identified as the
author of this work has been asserted in accordance with Section 77 of the Copyright, Designs
and Patents Act 1988

What Kingdom is No. 17 in the series New Scandinavian Literature

Graphic design by Rosie Ellison-Balaam
Printed by TJ Books, Cornwall, 2024

All rights reserved. Except for brief passages
quoted in a newspaper, magazine, radio, television, or website review, no part of this book may
be reproduced in any form or by any means, electronic or mechanical, including photocopying
and recording, or by any information storage and
retrieval system, without permission in writing
from the Publisher.

This translation was made possible through the generous support of the Danish Arts Foundation.

Danish Arts Foundation

A CIP catalogue record for this book is available from the British Library ISBN 978-1-915267-27-6

Lolli Editions
New Wing Exchange
Somerset House
Strand
London WC2R 1LA
United Kingdom
www.lollieditions.com